Ben Neihart

HEY, JOE

a novel

SIMON & SCHUSTER
New York London Toronto Sydney
Tokyo Singapore

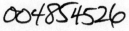

SIMON & SCHUSTER
Rockefeller Center
1230 Avenue of the Americas
New York, NY 10020

Copyright © 1996 by Ben Neihart
All rights reserved,
including the right of reproduction
in whole or in part in any form.

SIMON & SCHUSTER and colophon are registered trademarks
of Simon & Schuster Inc.

Designed by Kathryn Parise

Manufactured in the United States of America

10 9 8 7 6 5 4 3 2 1

LIBRARY OF CONGRESS CATALOGING-IN-PUBLICATION DATA

Neihart, Ben
Hey, Joe : a novel / Ben Neihart.
p.   cm.
1. Trials (Child sexual abuse)—Louisiana—New Orleans—Fiction.
2. Gay youth—Louisiana—New Orleans—Fiction.
3. New Orleans (La.) —Fiction.   I. Title.
PS3564.E296H49 1996
813'.54—dc20   95-43948
                        CIP

ISBN 0-684-81316-5

Part of this novel first appeared
in The New Yorker.

Acknowledgments

*I am especially grateful to Sloan Harris,
Sarah Pinckney, and Eric Steel.*

for Sharyn Rosenblum

A LATE-SUMMER
FRIDAY AFTERNOON

3 : 3 0   p . m .

Joe was newly sixteen. He had the rosy aspect, and the swagger, and the skinny arms, and the bad reputation. He was a brooder, a magazine reader, a swaying dancer at mellow, jazzy rap parties. He kept his hair cut short like the other smoked-out newbies at Metairie Park Country Day, and the only shoes he wore were black suede Pumas.

School had just let out for the Labor Day weekend, so Joe was home, changing clothes, in a hurry to be gone before his mother returned from work. He hated to leave her alone on a Friday night with her books and the cell phone. He hated the actual leave-taking most of all—her quick kiss, the sound of the front door's bolt lock when he closed it behind him. He wished she didn't spend so much time by herself. Why didn't she hang with her old friends? She was always working—at

Tulane Medical Center, in the fund-raising office, asking doctors and scientists and presidents of Corporation Whatever for money. "It's gonna suck the life right out of me," she sometimes joked. Joe hated her saying that, because he could see that it was true; in the past year, it seemed, skin and muscle hung more loosely on her frame, and on her face, even though she did exercises in the high-ceilinged ballroom of the New Orleans Athletic Center, downtown.

He wandered about the living room, looking for his glasses, which he wore only at home. They were hidden somewhere beneath the spoils of his mom's latest shopping spree. On the floor were neat piles of new compact discs, hardcover novels by Eurowomen with killer black hairdos, and shoe boxes. Slung over the furniture were silk blouses, palazzo pants in four shades of cream, and bras and panties, all of them with price tags still attached.

"And the value of this showcase is . . . ," Joe said, and then he hurried down the hall to the bathroom.

In his underwear, he crouched over the bathroom sink. It was his pond, shell shaped, with separate faucets for hot and cold water. The mirror was steamproof, and flattering; it put your face at a remove, so you weren't right on top of yourself as you did your routine. He squirted some Dial onto a washcloth and worked up a lather to freshen his underarms. He rubbed on some deodorant next, then washed his face and brushed his teeth.

He went into his mom's bedroom. As always, it was neatly set up for when she would come home this evening. The king-size bed was made; a pair of jeans and an immaculate white T-shirt and fresh panties lay on the pillow; the blinds were closed to keep the room cool in the late-summer sunlight. Joe liked the feel of the wood floor under his bare feet. He hopped onto the doctor's-office scale beside the dresser.

One hundred twenty pounds. Good, he told himself, you're keeping your shit lean and portable.

He pulled his mom's door shut on his way to his own bedroom, the smallest room of the house—even smaller than the bathroom. He liked the fact that when he lay down to sleep he could touch the walls on either side of his bed. On weekend mornings, his mom would come into the room to wake him up early so they could spend the morning together in the back yard, sitting on the stone benches in her little rock garden. Between them, they'd drink a pitcher of orange juice, and then Joe would go inside to fix enormous tumblers of iced tea, to clear the thickness from their throats. It was as if they hadn't missed each other in the comings and goings of the week. Long, contented silences; bare feet stretching in the dewy grass; the sun pumping higher into the sky.

Now Joe pulled the front off one of his waist-high Sony speakers, which had been hollowed out to hold his business, the top-shelf weed he imported from Gainesville and sold to his friends. He unrolled a Ziploc freezer bag and took a deep breath of the sweet, fearsome herb. He took a pinch to roll a quick joint. Time to give fashion, he thought. He lit up and collapsed onto his bed. He didn't have to turn on his stereo; music presented itself, as if it had lain dormant in the joint: "Nickel bag, a nickel bag . . ."

As he got stoned, he looked at his hands, which were covered with scars. His legs and feet were, too. Each scar was the proof of a mountain-bike tumble or, in one case, a skid across the coral beach on Fitzroy Island in the Great Barrier Reef, where they had gone last Christmas—Joe, his mom, and his dad, just before his dad died. They had pushed Daddy's wheelchair to the edge of the Coral Sea. "A sea like green milk," Daddy had said. Joe and his mom hurtled past the breaking waves and dove head on, grasping handfuls of water, racing, floating. When they were finished, they stood beside Daddy, dripping onto his sunburned legs and shoulders. "Oh," he said. "Oh, does that feel good."

■

Now Joe heard the mail truck stop outside. Friday was a magazine day. He drew himself out of bed, sprayed some Lysol around. He locked up the house and galloped down the driveway. The mailbox was rooted in a pile of pink, round stones. Joe kicked them with his toe. He left the bills and letters in the box and pulled out the new *Vogue*. He sat down on the slope of curb where his driveway met the street. He'd wait here a while, he decided, for his ride, Wyatt K., to pick him up and drive him to the Quarter, where it was their habit to spend Friday nights.

He set the magazine on his bare legs and took stock of the cover. The model was the angel of Joe's life. Her name was Linda, and the cattish regard of her eyes could pull you out of a funk. Joe had been following her career for five years now. In interviews, Linda said that all she had ever wanted to be was a model; she didn't want to be an actress or a singer or a politician, and she didn't want to talk about her charities or whatever, and she talked to her mom every day, and they talked about modeling, because that was Linda's job.

On this cover, Linda sat in the grass; she wore a grape velvet dress that was tight in the bodice. The lightest strands of her hair—the color of Coke in a glass full of melting ice—caught the sun, reminding Joe of the old Dutch society paintings that he had admired in his World of Art: The Netherlands class. In those paintings the background was usually dark—an inky, enamel cloud—to set off the lighter wires of the subject's hair and her lucent, honeycomb ruff and her knot of blue pearls.

He looked into Linda's eyes and tried to imitate her smile. "Wiggy wack," he said. He pressed his knees together and palmed the hair on his legs as if smoothing a skirt. Then he noticed the small type near the bottom of the cover: LINDA EVANGELISTA IN LOVE. He turned to the table of contents. He felt as if the boundary between his fingers and the page were disintegrating. There! He paged through the dark-hued Steven Meisel photographs, and then he stopped. A two-page spread of Linda, wearing a gray cropped sweater. She lay beneath her boyfriend, Kyle, the actor from *Twin Peaks*, on a blanket that was suffused with morning sunlight. They were kissing, openmouthed. Her hand—with polished, short nails—gently held the side of his neck.

"Work it, Linda," Joe said happily, and then he lay back on the driveway, holding the magazine to his chest. Music billowed from the house next door, where a former friend of his, Al Theim, lived—a Michael Bolton number, sung as if the singer had taken an Uplift enema. Joe howled along in a fake, sour-bellied voice: "Nothing cures your heart like time, love, and tenderness."

■

It was just like Al Theim to broadcast that kind of shit. Joe couldn't believe he'd once been in love with the guy. They used to spend afternoons together listening to Al's older brother's leftover records from the early eighties: A Flock of Seagulls, Visage, Ultravox. The singers wore makeup, and their hair was swept up in whoopie curls and banglets, but the songs, Joe thought, were some songs. Longing vocals on top of wet, sparkly keyboards: "Ultraviolet, radio lights, telecommunication . . ."

One warm October evening, almost four years earlier, Joe's mom had taken Joe and Al to Scream in the Dark, a haunted house set up in two gaping, connected barns, across the Mississippi in Algiers. Christian kids dressed from top to bottom in hunter orange directed the parking, took admission money, and made you sign an injury-release form. It felt like summer: it was seventy-four degrees out in the early evening. Joe and Al wore matching, tartan-plaid, flimsy cotton shorts. Even their thin, hairless legs matched.

"What kind of movie is this?" Joe's mom asked, bending over a picnic table to sign her form. Despite Joe's warning, she'd got herself up in a long black dress.

Joe went first, on his hands and knees into the entrance tunnel. Al followed, and then Joe's mom, her knees bound up in the dress. At the end of the tunnel was a ladder. Joe climbed to the second level, a pitch-dark room of indeterminate size, at the far end of which flashed the strobe-lit entrance to the next room. He ventured forward; Al and Mom followed.

"I thought it was going to be a movie," Mom said, and they all laughed. Then, in the dark, someone touched Joe's shoulder.

He shouted, "Al! That's not funny."

"I didn't do anything," Al whispered.

"Someone touched me," Mom said. "Run!"

Joe hurried through the lightlessness, his forearms braced in front of him, into the following room. The floors and walls and ceiling were painted in a black-and-white checkerboard pattern; the strobe light worked its distortions. Joe looked over his shoulder at his mom and laughed. She chanced a smile. The kids in front of him were trying to get to the other side of the room, but they couldn't walk straight. The floor was a sharp pyramid, and you slid backward as you got closer to the peak. Joe looked over his shoulder. The wall behind his mother was moving. There was a man in a checkerboard costume, face painted white, sliding along the wall. He reached out to touch her. Joe took her hand and dragged her into the next room.

Here, in a hyped-up jungle where the recorded sounds of squawking birds and giggling monkeys played deafeningly, Joe's mom disappeared; she had found the emergency exit and run out. Joe could hear her shouting, "I thought it was a movie!" The floor was made of foam rubber and covered with rolling, shin-high hurdles. Al took Joe's hand. A gorilla watched them from behind a vivid palm tree, the outline of which was glowing purple.

Al could distinguish the hurdles from the flat stretches, but Joe, at first, couldn't; he perceived, instead, only the fluo-rescent foliage painted on the foam. Al shouted "Jump!" at each hurdle.

There was nothing like holding Al's warm sweaty hand. At what looked to be the final hurdle, Joe made himself fall, and pulled Al with him. They wriggled to the wall, Joe's head propped on the foam hurdle, Al's head on Joe's chest. They watched the jumble of flapping shirts and jeans, listened to the screams and laughter.

Al touched Joe's face. "I like you," he said.

"I like you more than that," Joe said.

"How much?"

Their voices stayed in the space between their faces, and Joe found himself close to tears. "More than I like anyone," he said. "All day in school, I think about you." Birds called. The gorilla moved closer, then paused.

"Man, that makes me feel good," Al said. "Say it again."

And then there had been a kiss.

Now, spread out on his driveway, Joe shuddered and shut his eyes tight. The memory had returned with unwelcome carnal immediacy. Al Theim hadn't meant a word he said, Joe thought. Al Theim was just some wack softhearted guy who blew a few sentences out of his mouth. And so were the handful of guys he'd met since. Bullshitters. Maybe I'm not trying hard enough, he thought. Maybe tonight I'll talk to every person I see on Decatur Street, just bust up to them on the sidewalk and introduce myself. He shifted his head on its bed of grass clippings and loose gravel, and then he fell asleep.

He awoke to the whoop of an approaching car horn. He cracked open his eyes and just barely lifted his head to see who it was. A top-dollar car, reflecting sunlight, so he couldn't make out its color. Friends? Family? He dropped his head back and shut his eyes.

The car pulled onto the driveway beside him, purred for a moment, and then went silent.

The door opened, and his mother said, "Wake up, I'm home."

"Hey," Joe said.

She walked around the car, the soles of her low heels scratching the macadam. She came to his spot beside the mailbox and crouched down next to him. "Where you going tonight?"

"Out with friends."

"Okay, I won't ask." She settled onto her knees and smoothed her lemony cotton lap.

"I *said* out with friends."

"I *said* I won't ask."

Joe struggled to sit, propping himself up on one elbow. He looked at his mother's shoes, at her hose and her dress, at her knuckly hands and freckled arms—the freckles from long hours of weekend sunbathing. He knew why she liked the heat beating down on her, emptying her thoughts. He appreciated as much as she did the sensation of spilling a glass of iced tea down your throat as you lay, nearly still, on a chair in your own back yard.

Joe could tell that she was tired. It was Friday. It had been a long week. He put his hand on the side of her face. Her skin was soft, and cold from the car's A.C. "Stay with me a minute," he said. "Let's hang out for a minute."

She tilted her head to the side, catching his hand between her cheek and shoulder and holding it there. "You talk," she said. "I'd be so grateful."

∎

They lay side by side on the driveway, almost napping. Wyatt K., typically, hadn't shown up yet; the boy was always late.

Joe let his eyes flutter open and saw that his mom had begun to sweat through her dress, which was knee length, glittery lemon, with lace around the collar. Joe was moist, too; his T-shirt stuck to his chest and back. "Let's go inside," he said.

"Should we?"

"I think so."

"What'll we do?"

"There's a lot of stuff to do."

"Okay," she said, and opened her eyes. "I was mugged today."

Joe twisted onto his side, scraping his elbow on the rough macadam. He let out a whistley sigh. "Are you okay, Mom?"

"They both had guns," she said listlessly. "It was at the money machine. They made me withdraw the limit." She coughed and then drew herself up into a sitting position. "I don't know why they always pick on me."

"I don't either. Were you scared?"

"I still am."

Joe nodded, more to himself than to her. "I guess I'm scared, too. That it's happened to you like three times or whatever."

"But there's no lesson to learn from it. Believe me, I've tried to concoct one."

Joe smiled. "I'm sure you have." He jumped to his feet, helped her to hers.

They trudged up the driveway and went inside the house, where they fucked around for a little bit—Joe in his room, hitting a joint and watching the first minutes of a horror movie he'd made with his dad; Mom in her room, doing whatever.

After a while they ended up in the frosty kitchen, sitting at opposite ends of the glass-and-metal table. A dewy pitcher of iced tea sat in the center, and they each had a tall, cube-filled glass. The overhead light was turned off, but the drooping lower crescent of the sun shined directly into the small awning window above the kitchen sink; the room was bright.

Joe began to page through *Vogue;* he stopped on a black-and-white photo of Linda Evangelista, worked up in a shoe-length, hand-painted velvet robe, and her boyfriend, in tight pants and riding boots, stomping along an empty country road. The photo filled up Joe's head with a desperation to kiss someone. He made his eyes bear down on the crook of the boyfriend's elbow; it was looped tight across the dip where Linda's shoulder became her neck.

"I hate them," he said, and slammed the magazine shut. He looked up at his mom, whose face glowed with so much intimacy and delight that Joe looked back at the magazine. "I had gym today. We drove golf balls. I suck at it."

"You don't. That's something your father convinced you."

"No. I suck."

"If you do, it's one of very few things."

"You're wrong," he said gravely, and looked at his skinny forearm. He was impatient to get his weekend rolling; if nothing else, he had his heart set on smoking the fatty in his jeans pocket—smoke the whole thing all by himself, smoke it up. He wanted to brown his brain. But his ride was late. His boy, Wyatt K., was not on schedule, of course; nothing to do but wait for him. Whenever Joe called him to bug his ass and hurry him on his way, Wyatt got cranky and called Joe "Mommy."

"We should eat," Mom said, and put her head in the crook of her elbow, chin resting on the table. She had already removed all of her jewelry: watch, six rings, four bracelets, a silver chain that held a Danish krone. The clasps and settings glittered in a semicircle at the base of the iced-tea pitcher.

Joe smiled secretly at the booty; it reminded him that Daddy's pet name for Mom had been "Mrs. T." He saw his distorted reflection in a wide band of silver bracelet. He looked like E.T. "Okay, I'll make a salad."

"Check for produce. I don't know what we've got."

"Yes'm." He lifted up from his seat and took two giant steps to the refrigerator, pulled the door open. The shelves gleamed; they were immaculate and mostly empty, except for three cans of Sprite. The door was full of condiments: at least eight different mustards, a dozen salad dressings, regular and fat-free mayo, a gallon jug of ketchup, plastic lemons and limes, pickles, relishes, and a squeeze bottle of green poblano that he had bought at Taqueria Corona, his favorite restaurant, a meat-smoky taco café on Magazine Street, uptown.

His eyes traveled the interior, hopefully, expectantly, and then: bounty! The foggy plastic door of the crisper glowed with a promising condensation-speckled green. Joe pulled it open.

"Drumma: hit me!" he rasped. He grabbed hold of two heads of lettuce—one red-leaf, for flavor, and one iceberg, for crunch—seized a bag of baby carrots that looked like they might have wilted, half an onion wrapped in cellophane, a glossless yellow pepper, and three loose, rooty radishes. He spun around to set up a workplace beside the sink.

Mom pinged her iced-tea glass; the sound was formal and hollow. "Did I ask you how your presentation was today? Did you do okay?"

"Slam-kabam! Broken down perceptions limp limp *limp* out of the class, dignity fallin' off them. A new understannin', Miss Thing. Newbies congratsing me all afternoon as I strat down the hall. Check!"

After a moment, Mom said, "Should I be pleased?"

Joe was chopping radishes. "I made a theory or two. I eloquently presented said theory—about that painting I saw in Copenhagen. With Grandma. When you sent me away."

"I remember."

"You should."

"Which painting?"

"You know."

"Nope."

"Mom."

"Joe."

"You know which one I mean. You do."

"Remind me. I'm old."

Joe looked over his shoulder at her, narrowed his eyes. "Don't talk like that."

She didn't meet his gaze.

"It was a painting called *Dageraad der Gouden Eeuw*." The name, as it spilled from his mouth, summoned the afternoon that he and his grandmother had spent in the Louisiana Museum, on the beach, just across the water from Sweden.

Gallery upon gallery of wood and stone and paintings by aborigines. When your eyes got tired of art, you could look through the glass outer walls and meditate on the brown coast: rocks that looked like wood pummelled by foamy gray-green waves that disappeared in fog.

When he returned home from Europe, Joe found out that the vacation had coincided with his dad's first round of chemo treatment at Ochsner Clinic. Eight weeks on, then three off; six weeks on, a week off; and so on. Daddy was always cold. You could see a vein in his neck. As he lost his hair, he began to steal Joe's Saints and LSU ball caps.

"Did that painting have the moon shining on a dog?" Mom asked.

"No. It's all those buff angels floating against a dark background. I have it on a double-wide postcard. The angels hang real close to one another. Buff naked guy's in the center. Not hardly attenuated, not these angels."

"An enormous painting?" Mom asked diffidently and then laughed. "Was it heroic?"

"How big do you mean?" Joe tried to suppress a giggle as he rinsed lettuce.

"Big enough for Martha Stewart's living room?"

"I bet it is."

"Well let's buy it and ship it; Martha trusts our taste."

"What should we write on the card?"

"For our most precious angel . . ."

"Sick."

"For a woman who's always been there . . ."

Joe struggled with the yellow pepper, cutting away the seeds. He was trying to keep his head together, but it was hard. He didn't want a salad, didn't want a quiet dinner at home. No. Fuck that. He needed a song, a kiss, a bag of dope, a beer, his hand on the back of someone's neck.

Then he remembered that he was in a conversation.

"The cool thing to me," he blurted, "is that there are some suave fabrics draped around the body, like with piss-ignorant embroidery and gold leaf and piping. And then, in this one corner, the black background is rubbed away or whatever, and the background that remains is lighter."

"Mmmm."

"In that light corner there's a castle. Maybe all those bodies floated out of the castle windows. Do you know what I'm saying? Like, those bodies are balloons, and they were in storage in the castle, and somebody opened a window and they escaped. Or maybe that's stupid. Maybe it's a trivial-type analysis. But don't like worry, because that's not at all the way I presented myself in school. I was Mr. Overpreparation, just like I guess you always told me. Okay?" He stopped talking, found the plastic, everyday salad bowls in the dishwasher; they were flipped on their bottoms and puddled with detergenty water. He rinsed them in the sink, pulled the Paul Newman dressing from the fridge, and then he loaded the salad, plates, napkins, and silverware into his arms. He turned toward the table.

His mom was asleep, her breath rasping lightly, steadily. He couldn't tell if she was pretending.

"Mom," he whispered.

No answer.

"Hey," he whispered again. "Hey, Mom." When she didn't stir, he passed into the dining room, set up a place for himself at the peeling white table. He thought about finding his Walkman for some dinner music, but he knew that he'd be buzzing too loud and maybe he wouldn't hear the phone or his ride—stupid, conceited, tall Wyatt K.—horn-honking out in the driveway.

Eating dinner alone was something you got used to. You did it and you did it, and you started to eat maybe louder than you were supposed to, and you didn't really keep your mouth exactly closed when you chewed, and you used your fingers.

There had been all those weeks when Daddy couldn't keep anything in his stomach. Or Mom would go straight from her office to Daddy's private room in the same hospital. Or Joe would be at school late, watching some newbies practice soccer, or he'd play squash at the New Orleans Athletic Center with Wyatt K. or Shelby Jahncke and get home after dinner. Even before Daddy actually died, it had gotten to the point where Joe didn't want a family dinner—not even on a special occasion, a holiday, good news, Mom's one decent mood of the week. Even last Christmas, when they were on an island off the north coast of Australia, and they were sort of trying to come to terms with the fact that Daddy was going to die or whatever, Joe had made sure that he'd eat alone. He'd wait until after dark to come home from the coral beach, where he'd lounged all day.

You had to hike through a rain forest to get back to the hotel—up over plates of rock, hoisting yourself with gummy-stalked vines. The trail followed the curves of the shoreline, so the ocean was just a few dozen yards away; you'd hear its hushed breakers. Above, there were canopies of overlapping leaves. There were swarming bugs with steel blue wings; they'd sink toward Joe, even brush his cheeks and the back of his neck before returning to their high perches.

On the night before the family was to fly back to New Orleans, the march through the rain forest didn't slow him down as much as he wanted it to, so he plopped down on the end of the pier where the snorkeling and diving boats were tied up. The sun had just gone down—in a hurry, as if it had been swallowed whole. The sky was like the inside of a licorice jelly bean: black, with hard, sugary ridges. His bathing suit was still damp and sandy; every time he shifted his ass on the rough wood of the dock, the fabric chafed his dick, not really unpleasantly.

He sighted a cane fire burning across the ocean on the mainland, and got lost in its reds and yellows, and meditated on the day that had just passed. He had baked most of the day, asleep on a thin towel that was spread over the sharp coral. Finally, just before sunset, he'd hobbled to the limpid green water's edge, slid down a yard-high bank of the dead, bleached bones into the warm sea. Submerged, he took a gulp of salt water and let himself drift out into the abyssal calm.

Now he looked at the fiery horizon. It was like a distant commemoration of his good day. The wet, briny breeze hung tight to his head and bare back. He could picture his parents eating dinner in bed, watching TV, Mom stopping every once in a while to wipe Daddy's brow with one of the deep blue washcloths from the hotel bathroom.

A hand gripped his shoulder and squeezed. "You want a beer?"

Joe looked up behind him at the ridges of a man's smooth belly and chest. He worked his eyes up the neck. It was Pieter, a guy he'd met—but just barely—at the beach today. He was Dutch, but he'd grown up in Los Angeles. Or so he'd told Joe before sauntering in the direction of three topless women arranged around a big black rock's blowhole, farther down the shoreline.

"Yeah," Joe said cautiously, "beer'd be cool." Pieter's hospitality was a little suspect; he had the asshole face of a mean Californian. He was cute—skinny, taller than Joe, short black hair, fat lips—and there was no way he was maybe into guys or bisexual or whatever.

Joe tried to concentrate on how to *be*. He didn't want to act too shy and victimy or too boisterous and eager. He wanted to be the mellow, stoned guy that nobody fucks with because what's the point, the guy's so baked and stupid.

Just deal, he told himself. Whatever.

Pieter sat down, settled against him, shoulder and arm and thigh pressed to Joe's. He was drunk. Sunburned, too. His sand-crusted skin was giving off heat. Joe's muscles and nerve endings went on automatic alert; his dick got achy hard.

Perfect. He closed his eyes and tried to wish himself home. That's real well done, he said to himself. Then he sprung his eyes open, looked sideways at Pieter's knuckles where they gripped the dock, and set about planning an escape.

"I feel good, my man," Pieter said; his feet splashed abruptly into the water and disappeared. He dug into his backpack, popped open two cans of Foster's, handed one to Joe, and started talking about some of the girls who'd been down at the nude beach. "Titty hard-on, that German chick. You see her thighs?"

"Which girl was she?"

"The German!"

"I don't know who you mean."

"Fuckdelicious."

"Yeah?"

"I *thought* you were jes a boy," Pieter laughed. "How old are you—thirteen or something?"

"Fifteen."

"Fifteen? You sure you're not lying?"

"Yeah?"

"I'm eighteen."

"Cool."

Waves swept against the dock pilings. The small boats strained out into the current, yanking their tie ropes. The sky was black, but toward the mainland it reflected some of the orange and white of the cane fires.

"I wanna get tweaked," Pieter said.

"Go right ahead," Joe said. "I grant you immunity from prosecution."

The Dutch boy giggled to himself and then he leaned imperceptibly closer to Joe. "I accept your kind offer, sir," he murmured in a winky little voice.

Behind the dock and back some distance, music emanated from the hotel's outdoor bar. It was twinkly, forgotten U.S. dance music by a foxy white redhead who had the same moves as Janet Jackson. Joe couldn't remember her name, but he remembered dancing to this song at a sixth-grade dance. "You give me a good vibe / don't you know baby . . . ," she sang. As Joe sucked on his beer, head back, he allowed his shoulders to roll in time to the beat.

When the song ended, he said, "I used to like that."

"That's a faggoty song," Pieter said with finality.

"Yeah." Joe winced. "It is. I used to like it."

"Used to be a fag, huh?"

Joe looked at the glinting water; for a moment, he considered dropping into the tender-looking chop. "I guess I was."

"No way!" Pieter bellowed, turning his face toward Joe.

"Yep."

"You grew out of it."

"I hope," he said slowly. Lightheaded, he leaned back and rested on his elbows. He shut his eyes. "Can I have another beer?"

"Sure, dude." Pieter set his backpack on his lap and rummaged in it. "Got plenty. They're not so cold anymore."

"I hope I'm not bringing you down."

"I'm at the Great Barrier Reef," Pieter sputtered with high spirits, holding up a can of beer so it was backlit by the moon. He popped it open and handed it to Joe. "I saw the sunset. I always wanted to come here, but I was never sure I'd make it. You can't count on luxury shit to happen."

"I know. But it's nice when it does, huh."

"That's straight up. Can't count on getting laid, either, but the German girl's meeting me here in an hour." Pieter approximated a full-throated dog growl. "She's going to lock my face between her thighs . . ."

Joe held the warm can to the side of his face. "What does it taste like, guy?"

"Oh, man." Pieter began to shake with silent laughter. "Oh, man."

"You can't tell me?"

"I'm not that interested in explaining it."

"That's sucky," Joe said before he could stop himself. "Selfish." He didn't know what else to do, so he leaned forward and dropped off the dock into the warm, gasoline-scented water.

"Overboard," bellowed Pieter.

The chop lapped and swelled around Joe's shoulders. He floated in place for a moment and then dunked underwater. He swam along the side of one of the diving boats, keeping his eyes shut so he wouldn't spot imaginary barricuda and jellyfish. When he resurfaced, he let himself bob to the boat's rhythm.

"Where are you?" Pieter called out in a hearty, eager voice. "How's the water?"

"It's nice," Joe answered.

"D'ya want me to come in? Y'wanna race?"

"Um . . . *no.*"

"Come back, then. Keep me company."

Joe glided closer to shore and got a foothold on the silty bottom. "I gotta head to the hotel, dude. You keep yourself company."

"Ah, come back," Pieter groaned.

Joe dragged his feet through the dry sand until they were coated, and then he jogged along the gravel path that led to the hotel. He sat for a minute on the wooden bench outside the entrance, looked at the cloud sacs that bulged down out of the sky. Then, still a little bit drunk, he pushed through the glass double doors, waved to the front-desk girl, and swayed down the dim corridor toward the room he shared with his parents. Locked.

He knocked; then twice; then a third time before the door finally opened.

The overhead lights were on; it took a few seconds for his eyes to adjust.

The suntanned, redheaded doctor who'd visited every day was sitting on the bed beside Joe's father's body, which was covered to the neck with a sheet. Daddy's face and hair looked wet.

"Honey," said Mom, standing just inside the door. She let go of the knob, took Joe's hand, ushered him inside. "He's gone. We watched out the windows so he could see the water." She pulled him against her.

"I'm sorry I wasn't here," Joe said. He looked over his mother's shoulder out the window, and then the crying started.

■

The dining room was still sunny, but now, suddenly, the house was too coldly air-conditioned. Joe's arms were goosefleshed.

No, he ordered himself. The tears that had threatened shrank back into their ducts. He looked up from the table, out the French doors and onto the back lawn. There, next door, was Al Theim—shirtless—playing Nerf football with his big sister, Messy.

Messy held the ball expertly in front of her and punted it over Al's head; as he lifted his arms to reach for it, his flat belly collapsed inward, making a cave. When he recovered the ball, he drew his arm back and threw a nice spiral. Joe's gaze traveled down Al's shoulder, lingering on the crook of his elbow.

Fuck, Joe said to himself, I could get a life.

He shot up from the table and took his dishes into the kitchen. He scraped the soggy bottom layer of the salad bowl—he'd eaten the whole thing without meaning to—into the disposal and threw the plates and silver into the dishwasher. Then he turned to his mother.

"Mom," he said in a low voice. "Hey, Mom."

She stayed asleep, breathing heavy and regular.

"Mom," he said a little more loudly.

Her eyes crinkled open and focused on him. "I was asleep."

"Yeah."

"Did you already eat?"

"Yeah."

"Did I?"

"Yeah."

"Liar."

"I'm not."

"Joe." She lifted her head from the table. "I'm going to stand up."

"Oh."

"And then I'm going back to my room to lie down. A nap. I brought some work home for tonight." She groaned as she rose to her feet. Her shoulders were pushed forward, and the side of her face that she'd slept on was puffy and red. The lap of her dress was full of creases.

"You have to eat something, Mom. Come on."

"I'm fat." She smoothed her palm across her forehead.

"So."

She laughed, shoulders wiggling. "I'm not, am I?"

As Joe moved closer to her, he felt momentarily huge. Even though he was only a few inches taller than she was, he could look down on the top of her head and have an unsympathetic thought about the slightly crooked, vulnerable part in her black hair. He had an urge to weep. "I wish you wouldn't go to bed already," he said. "Why do you have to?"

She moved her gaze to the floor and drew her feet together.

"Mom, it's depressing to be in the same house. I feel like I have to tiptoe around or I'll disturb you. It's like death in here; it really is."

"Don't say that."

"Daylight, and you're asleep. God." The words came out as if tiny flares were attached to their ends. He bit his upper teeth down hard on the lowers until the muscles in his jaw ached.

"It hurts my feelings and not only that."

"What." Another flame, more smoke.

"I don't decide on my way home from work that I'm going to come home and collapse," she said delicately. "It's hardly my intention. But I still have raw feelings, Joe. It is a relief for me to fall asleep."

"Is it *me?* Do you get upset when you see me?"

"What a question! Of course it hurts me. Of course it does."

"Would it help if I stayed away all evening and then just sort of snuck in?"

The muscles of her face relaxed into a smile. "All day, I look forward to getting home and talking with you. I can't think of anything better for me, even if I still get overwhelmed."

"I can't be any more of that, not all of the time," Joe said.

"Why? What's wrong with the way you are with me?"

"It makes me crazy inside!" With the side of his fist, he pounded the wall. "It's like, if I'm not nice to you, then who will be? That's what I think about. Am I supposed to be your like best friend?"

"You *are*, though." Her eyes glistened. "That's just the way it is."

"No," he said. "No, no, no. Wyatt K. is my best friend. And after that it's Shelby."

"This isn't a good time for me to talk," she said, and as she moved wordlessly past him she seemed to flinch before going into her bedroom and clicking the door quietly shut behind her.

He heard the first high notes of her sobbing, and his own face crumpled in response. The hall stretched in front of him reproachfully, as if it were an appendage of her closed door that would lift off its foundation and batter him against the wall. He walked softly to his own room. He shut his door, dropped onto his mattress, walked on his knees to the window. Why am I so mean? he asked himself. Should I just buy a gun and shoot her, is that what I want to do? He pressed his forehead against the glass; it was warm. He shut his eyes, trying not to think of anything. The air-conditioning vent was on the floor beneath him; its cold breeze fluttered against the front of his thighs and the underside of his chin.

When he opened his eyes, he had an intuition of movement just outside his vision. He repositioned his face, cheek to glass, so that he had a view—however askew—of Al Theim's yard. Mr. Energy himself chased his sister across the grass; with every stride, the muscles in his back writhed beneath the skin. As he caught up to her, she turned to face him, arms flopping at her sides. He wrapped his arms around her, his front to hers, and lifted her, and then fell forward with her in a kind of tackle.

Joe sighed to himself, put a dramatic hand to his forehead, and fell backwards on his mattress.

■

Ten minutes later, Joe was knocking on her door. "Mom," he called, "what are you doing? Do you wanna watch this video with me?"

"Come in."

He creaked the door open and stepped just inside the room. "I didn't mean all the stuff I said. It was really selfish of me."

"Don't even worry," she said. "We both need to let it out."

"Yeah, I think we do."

"So we're in agreement."

The room was shadowy except for the outside light coming in the window beside her bed. She had a stack of work papers beside her.

"You have that concentrating look," he said. "You're doing hospital crap?"

"Yeah."

"You have enough for the whole weekend?"

"Well, I don't know. There's always *enough*."

"Sure."

She held out her palm. "Put the movie in, honey. I'd love to watch it."

"Is your VCR working okay?"

"I think so."

He walked over to the bed, sat on the edge, and bent forward to put the tape in. He pulled the remote from the top of the TV and lay back, helping himself to a handful of cashews from a jar that lay on its side in the surf of bedcovers. "Sal-ty." He laughed.

"Sur-prise." She giggled.

He looked over his shoulder at her. "Crank-y."

"Not anymore," she said lightly, and smiled as if a blue jay had just landed on her shoulder.

"Cool if I click the mother on?"

"Sure."

The blue screen disappeared and was replaced by the first, precredits, scene. Joe, as an intoxicated teenager, lay on a stone bench in the backyard. Daddy, dressed as a priest, performed the rites of exorcism.

Joe moved his lips along with the words his dad said on screen: "How long, Lord? Wilt thou be angry forever? Shall thy jealousy burn like fire?" His shoulders tightened in anticipation of what would happen next, and then it did: a dire shadow passed across Joe's on-screen face, and the scene ended, and the credits began. It had taken his dad almost the whole weekend to edit that scene just right.

The entire movie lasted half an hour; in it there were two more exorcisms, several more intense passages that Joe had chosen from the book of Psalms, and a little bit of gore. There were two scenes in the backyard, two in Joe's bedroom (done up with aluminum foil and black sheets), and one scene just inside the front door. It wasn't the worst piece of shit Joe'd ever sat through, but he knew that no one but him and his mom would ever want to sit around like this, watching it from beginning to end, enraptured.

5:15 p.m.

Seth Michaels was heavy in the shoulders. He was tapered at the waist. He was twenty-six, with diffuse goals, and he was still led by his prong in most of his actions. This afternoon, as a deliberating juror on dinner break, he was sequestered in the Holiday Inn across the street from the civil court building. The first court trial of his life!—and tonight, if all went well, there'd be a verdict.

He stood at the window naked, looking out. The afternoon sky was the color of plum flesh. Rain gushed down the streets, overflowing onto the swirl of lawn in front of the hotel. Traffic signals tossed in the wind, and an occasional spark of lightning photographed the skyline. Fury, fury, he thought to himself, pulling back his gaze, fixing his eye on the window glass itself and his reflection. The beauty of his arm lay in its many contrasts: the muscle mass of his biceps beneath soft pale skin; the leaner, twitching forearm muscles beneath wiry black hair. He tensed his fist a few times, admiringly, and then looked down at the scene below him. Three satellite trucks were parked on the sidewalk. A dozen or so reporters, holding umbrellas that were emblazoned with their stations' call letters, huddled together. City and court police mingled beneath the hotel's taxi awning.

"Come back to bed."

"Oh," he drawled, "we were in the middle of something." He turned away from the window, letting the curtain fall back into place. He stood motionless, letting his eyes adjust to the dark.

"I got to get back to my room before long," the woman juror murmured. "Let's finish."

"Can you see me?"

"It's not *that* dark, baby."

"I want you to make me hard."

"Come over here and I will."

"No. From there. With me standing here."

She groaned. "Don't play me."

"I want you to be helpless."

"*Right.*"

"You're so weak you can't speak."

"Are you serious?"

"You're drifting in and out of consciousness."

"No."

His heart stirred at her refusal. "Just lie still. Breathe. Let me listen. Five minutes."

She tossed around in the sheets, and after a moment whispered, "Okay."

Her name was Rita Ledet, and it had been Seth's intention to secure her Not Guilty vote. *Had been.* He had marked her at the very moment he first saw her in the jury-pool room.

She'd worn a willing, cynical face, so he'd sat beside her, flirted with her, spoke to her with deep respect, *listened* to her, and discovered that he'd judged her correctly. Rita was a lonely woman who watched too much TV and paid close attention to the stories in which everyday people lucked into huge sums of money. She seemed not to differentiate between those who won the lotto and those who filed improper lawsuits and those who accepted bribes. The last had been Seth's ambition. He was supposed to pull her by the throat into his tank of filth.

But today, during deliberations, he'd finally decided not to. He didn't want her vote; and now he was happy just to finish their negotiations here in the room and be done with her. Call it another step toward home. He would leave New Orleans tonight without reaching his goal of knocking every pretty ass the city offered. Rita was his consolation, he guessed: a thin-limbed dainty whose body folded beneath his like oversized butterfly wings.

He swaggered to the side of the bed. "What kind of music do you like, Rita?" he asked, prong in hand.

Excellent girl that she was, she didn't answer.

After a moment, he dropped onto the bed with exaggerated force; Rita's slim body lifted off the mattress for one sweet moment, and when she landed Seth lifted her shoulders up onto his kneeling lap and bent forward to kiss her. "I love you," he whispered into her hair as it fanned across his thighs. "You can't die, honey; don't die on me, dear." His giddy testicles had contacted their friends, the synapses along his spine; the frantic conversation, the exultations, reverberated in his ears.

"I feel so weak," Rita said, remaining perfectly still. "I'm so helpless." There were beads of sweat across the front of her chest, and in spatters on her nipples, and an eyedropperful topping off the elegant cup of her belly button. She blew a mouthful of air: "I'm scared."

"I could let you die," he said, nearly weeping, his face hanging just above hers. He swiped a finger along her shoulder, drew a parallelogram. He put the finger in his mouth, and it swelled on his tongue as if to choke him. "Your pulse is getting weaker. I think it's time." He shoved her gently from his lap and rolled on top of her, his full weight behind his knees, pressing into the mattress on either side of her pelvis.

He pulled his face abruptly away from her, weepily caught his breath, and then slid his mouth up the front of her body. He used his chest and one arm to pin her to the mattress as he licked the curls of hair along the side of her face. Stripping the oil from one thick lock—as if meat from a bone—he took a mouthful of the next, until the side of her head was matted with his spit. He closed his mouth over her ear, held it gently with his teeth like a bite of apple before you break the peel. As she turned her head away from him he released the ear; the sight of it glistening with his saliva gladdened him as if in some small way he had just given birth.

Mine. My secret. It was one of many.

Seth wasn't here by accident. He'd been paid $50,000 to seat himself on the jury. It was a civil case brought by the Lady Rampart orphanage against its former patron, the Myrtha Murphy Shaw Foundation—named for the trust's chairwoman, a coffee heiress. Seth's job was to hang the jury, thereby giving Rae Schipke, Mrs. Shaw's henchwoman, enough time to clean out her bank accounts and flee the country. Upon completion, he'd get another $50,000. An outright reprieve was worth half a million, but even under civil law, which required only nine votes for a verdict, that would be impossible.

The first problem was that Lady Rampart was a model institution, beloved in the city. The boys who lived there, full of vigor and self-discipline, were supported by the mayor, the city council, nearly every church and TV station. If it hadn't been for police misdeeds, Seth was sure that Schipke would have been convicted during the initial criminal trial last year, and thrown to the wolves. But cops had searched without warrants and fudged some of their sworn testimony, and the district attorney's case had fizzled in open court. With the civil suit, the orphans were ripping for a jackpot to compensate.

Second, Schipke was fucked in the head. She sat in court dressed in remorseless leather or silk, as if there weren't three lurid charges against her: sexing up a handful of the older boys at the orphanage, using foundation money to keep them quiet, and most damning, molesting two eleven-year-old boys whom she'd had to her home for weekend sleepovers. On each point, there'd been credible testimony, descriptions of the wispy growth of hair and arc of moles around Schipke's genitalia; in fact, the only witness in Schipke's defense had been Mrs. Shaw, who offered an improbable alibi for the nights on which the molestation had been alleged to occur. Shaw had grown up with Schipke's late mother, and treated Rae like a daughter.

The third problem was that Seth hated Schipke for what she had helped him make of himself, and had needed only the least stirring of his withered conscience to let her hang.

Now Rita whispered, "You're crushing me."

"I know. I can't help myself. I want to destroy you."

"I can't breathe."

"Try," he said, propping himself on his elbows, bearing his hips down on her.

She blew wet breath on the hollow at the base of his throat.

"O-kay," he said, and as he gruntingly slid down her body and began to slip his dick back inside her, she worked her arm free and took a handful of his neck. She inched fingers up the peak of his jaw and dug her nails into his lips. "What's this?" he asked.

She used her other arm to pressure him off her, and she rolled with him so that he lay on his back and she straddled his waist. "You're losing blood," she said. "You're drifting out. You can't speak."

"Save me," he panted. "Please help me."

■

Jury duty was the biggest gig that he'd pulled for Schipke, but it was hardly the first, nor did he take it more seriously than his many earlier chores. He'd become her job boy without regret or shame or gravitas.

It had happened like this: In ascending to the position of executive director of Shaw, a foundation whose assets had leaped past $100 million during the 1980s, Schipke had broken some backs. She was someone who kept track of her enemies and wished to lash them. For that certain kind of help, she'd turned to her lawyer, Darcy Favrot. He had his own firm, and also taught a class in ethical rhetoric at Tulane's Freeman School of Business, where one of his students was Seth Michaels. Darcy had an intuition, based on the mercenary voice of Seth's class papers, and arranged the Michaels-Schipke introduction. It was five years ago that Seth began as an intern. Rae hired him, and trained him—subtly for the first month, but once he caught on she ushered him without hesitation into her world.

He started off snooping for license plate numbers on Audubon Place, the private, guarded street where the presidents of banks, mineral companies, and restaurant chains lived. Rae had only wanted to know who was visiting whom, which forces in town were excluding her from their dinners, but Seth gave her more. He worked through the night, accessing public records on computer databases until he'd compiled financial portraits of the owners of each car. The next morning, he gave the notes to Schipke.

"This ought to be illegal!" she said and did a touchdown strut, flapping papers above her head.

Within a month, she had filled Seth's head with all of her grandiose apocalyptic musings. They'd begun having sex in her office late at night. She asked him to take on meaner chores. She increased his salary.

He broke into the Tulane and Loyola fund-raising offices to photocopy alumni files, which included records of stock holdings, assessments of property values, and other helpful documents. He telephoned anonymous threats to zoning board and city council members. He flattened tires, broke windows. For two years, he performed bad deeds in modest daily increments.

But in the fourth year he made the mistake of letting himself be thrilled by the fear his actions caused, and he got carried away. There were victims, hurt seriously: Nonie Daniels, of the Carthage Mill Company, whom Seth ambushed outside her back door one night and knocked unconscious; and Drew Oostdaam, the daughter of an NOPD beat cop, who cowered on the floor of her butt-ugly new Mustang as Seth shattered its windows with a tire iron. And his final target, the one who almost died, was a righteous good guy named Jim Yonce, a first-year law student investigating the foundation on behalf of the Citizen Law Clinic. Schipke hated him because she couldn't stop him from organizing every pussy little radical in town for the fight against the so-called exploitative and antiprogressive forces that Shaw funded.

When Seth was through with him, Yonce had to enter the hospital, and then a rehab facility.

Soon thereafter, Seth gave Schipke his notice. They whittled an understanding: he'd keep his mouth shut and so would she; she'd pay him for another year, or until he left town. Seth didn't hear from her until one vaporous night this summer, when he was in bed with a young thing he wanted to impress. Schipke called. She told him she had one more job for him.

"This is the big one," she said. "Nothing physical."

"How big?"

"This is real fresh pussy. You're first on my list."

"Tell it to me."

She told him that she had taken the liberty of calling a hacker friend of hers who knew the city's computer systems. This friend had checked Seth's name against the register of potential jurors and made an adjustment. Furthermore, Rae said, certain lawyers were predisposed to Seth's serving.

"You're a bona fide candidate," Rae said. "There's a letter on its way from City Hall. I hope you'll say yes."

"Yes," Seth said.

■

Seth buried his face in her belly as she straddled his face. He tasted minerals, oily and sweet and stony. He could taste his own humusy bouquet. He cried out in terror and kicked his feet up from the mattress as a near-orgasm spasm bent his insides.

"Slow down, baby," she said. "I'll have to give you a sedative."

"No," he whispered, "far too much danger. I'm not healthy, I'm not healthy enough."

"You seemed so healthy, white boy. All of them whites at

the start, during jury selection, and it come down to you and two yats who can't read. All of them others had excuses; they didn't want to drive into the city. Stay their asses out in Kenner." She took his chin in her damp fingers and moved his head so their eyes met. She bobbled her face down toward him and laughed; a bubble of her humid breath coated the inside of his throat. "But you stayed on. Why's that? What is it that you want from Rita?"

Seth cracked his mouth open into a grin. "Pussy?"

"Bitch!" She slapped his cheek.

Seth made a high sigh. The root of his balls sparkled all the way up inside his lower back. His chest, with her ass sitting right on it, was more sensitive and communicative than he'd ever have imagined; it alone pumped an extra couple of pints down into his prong. "Who voted me foreman, honey?"

"I didn't."

"Who'd you vote for?"

"Me."

"Fuck if I would."

After they came, Seth for the second time, he rolled onto his back and Rita used his belly for a pillow. The room was entirely dark; its smells were as in the back of a cave. The air above the bed was dark and speckled white as if with stars.

"Honey?" he said. He liked the way this felt, her supple cheek resting on him, rising and falling with his breath.

"Mmmm," she murmured.

"Do you want to know how I'm going to vote?"

"Y'already said in deliberations," she said with a hitch of suspicion.

"I know what I said. But I have to tell you something. I was being like truly the devil's advocate. I was wrong."

She lifted her head off him, and the skin on his belly felt

cooler, as it did when he took off his shirt after a gym work-out. "What are you gonna tell me?" It was true. There was almost disappointment in her voice.

"I think Rae Schipke's guilty."

"You do? But what about—"

"I do."

"And that's how you're going to vote?"

"It is," he said. "It is." A spray of laughter drifted from his mouth and floated to the ceiling. Rain beat against the windows. Softer than the rain, farther away, sirens spun.

"So am I," Rita said.

"We'll both have clean consciences then."

"Truly." Now she sounded relieved.

■

Alone now beneath his stained covers, Seth realized with dread that he didn't want to leave the motel room's dark, sterile calm. The drapes were absurdly heavy. The pastel paintings on the walls soothed. Even the feel of the crispy, chemically clean carpet on his bare feet was reassuring. Maybe, he thought, now that he was going to have to leave town in a rush—tonight, if he wanted to be sure of avoiding Schipke's wrath—he'd be living in hotels for a little while. He would like that.

He had gotten so close to fixing the jury. The first two marks had come so easily. In deliberations, they had turned to Seth with misplaced affection and admiration and taken at full value his claims that Mrs. Shaw's alibi for Schipke was reasonable, that the children had been coached to lies by social workers. As if he were the foundation's publicist, Seth had presented an argument that the foundation was above reproach because of the beautiful work it had done in restoring the orphanage building to its original splendor. Seth's marks had also gotten all tangled up in the judge's instructions about a "preponderance" of the evidence—curlicues, Seth thought, scrim work.

This morning, in secret ballots, the tally had stood at eight to four, with Seth, his two marks, and a fourth, whose identity he suspected—Rita?—but was still unsure of, blocking a conviction. The judge, in a calm written note responding to their standstill, had ordered the jurors to make one last try for a verdict before he declared a hung jury.

In less than an hour, Seth would get in the van and head back to the court building. He would change his vote. Perhaps, he thought, he could begin to change his ways.

■

The telephone rang. He threw his arm onto the bedside table and snatched the clunky receiver from its cradle. "Hello?"

"Hello." A wisp of a voice.

"Who is this?"

"Count your fingers and toes."

The skin across his shoulders and down his spine tingled. "Who is this?"

"Count your teeth."

"Who the fuck—"

"Seth!" A high, girly squeal, then sucking laughter.

"Tell me who this is."

"Death did to me short warning give . . ."

Who?

"They'll find you hanging from the ceiling." The caller hung up.

Seth held the dead receiver against his chest for a moment before he got out of bed and plodded across the carpet to the far window. He pulled the curtain aside a few inches. Rain was skidding sideways, spattering against the glass. Down below, the media stood in lighted clumps, setting up for the dull footage they liked to shoot of the backs of the jurors being escorted to the vans. The judge, Seth guessed, had already announced that one way or another the trial would end tonight.

Away from the motel, toward the Quarter, work-duty prison inmates in orange coveralls erected crowd barricades for this evening's parade, the first of the new Labor Day weekend festival that the city was promoting as an upstart, late-summer Mardi Gras—funky, the mayor's office said, but without the racist history. Seth had done some freelance phoners and mail drops for the festival publicists, some packaged TV news puff spots, all of it good work, a testament to his camaraderie with the city's ascendant political powers.

The inmates tossed the barricades off truck beds, then chained them together along the curb. Bend over, lift, toss; catch, place, chain. Easy work for a prisoner, Seth thought; the fencing was lightweight metal, carnival grade. Just as the sight of the underworked prisoners started to inflame his temper, his eye was drawn to a lighted set: four cameras and a couple of reporters across the street from the motel in front of the narrow cement rectangle that announced the courthouse parking facility.

Being interviewed were five of the older orphans from Lady Rampart. Seth recognized them by their bald heads and matching construction boots. He had to give it to them; they'd scored a dramatic backdrop: tufted, stumpy palm trees waggling in the wind beneath a clearing sky of blue-black clouds shot through with orange and red. Seth watched until the boys had finished their say. As they piled into their Jeep and drove away, he let the curtain close.

6:00 p.m.

Sometimes, Wyatt K. was Joe's best friend. He was good for all the guy activities that you could fit into a day. Like mountain biking on the trail that ran beside the Mississippi River, or driving up and down Airline Highway in the early evening, chilling to an onslaught of metallic, whining Beastie Boy rhymes, or smoking a fatty in Joe's bedroom before school. But there were other times—*plenty* of them—when Joe couldn't help but think of Wyatt K. as an opponent, a quarry, someone to fuck with and beguile.

Wyatt had just called to say that all of a sudden his parents were taking him to Houston for the Labor Day weekend. He was trying to be sincere, but he didn't have any of the right words.

Joe was letting him bumble. He listened in silence as Wyatt listed the places he was going to visit.

Astroworld.

One modern art museum. Didn't remember the name. Wyatt thought it was Joe's kind of thing more than his own. It was, but still Joe didn't say anything.

Three malls.

The sloppiest Tex-Mex restaurants, where he was going to smother his tacos in the greenest, pulpiest poblano.

Rice University, where Wyatt's dad had gone and where he wanted Wy to go, too, and play soccer, and turn himself into an electrical engineer.

"Joe—you there?" Wy asked. He sounded as if he'd just taken a bite of banana.

Joe didn't answer.

"I'm *sorry*, boy. I didn't *want* to bag on our plans."

"Whatever."

"Okay, I won't go. What do you want from me, boy?"

"It's okay, Wy. I'm sorry for acting like a wussy."

"Someone else can give you a ride to the Quarter. Call Shelby."

"I probably won't go. It's not like I was that into it."

"What are you gonna do, then?"

Joe was looking out his bedroom window. "Hang with my mom. Talk on the phone. Rent a movie. Give fashion." There was nothing going on in the neighborhood. Lawn sprinklers swirled. Chubby husbands and wives took power walks, slicing their arms through the air. The sun was orange with a few dots of red, like a fertilized egg yolk.

"Don't smoke it all up," Wy said. "Save some for me."

"You know I will," Joe said, and rolled onto his stomach. "I always do."

"Yeah . . ."

"That's the thing. I'm always good, boy. To you. I'm always a good friend to you."

"This is totally sick. You're making me feel bad."

"I'm not trying to."

After a brief pause, Wyatt said, "Maybe you are."

"You talk like that all the time. Just to make me feel like shit."

"Shut up."

"Whatever," Joe said. "Are you taking your skateboard?"

"My dad says I can't."

"I thought your dad was cool."

"He's pretty cool, but he wants this to be like my kind of mature side. To be convinced that I can handle it at Rice. Be in Houston or whatever. Because he thinks this city's for shit now and isn't gonna get any better."

"That's bullshit. I don't ever wanna live some other city."

"I don't know. I don't think about it. Well, sometimes I do. Maybe there aren't gonna be any opportunities when we get out of college. That's what my dad says."

"Your dad who won't let you pack a totally packable skateboard in your suitcase."

"Yeah. Him."

"Sucks. Some sweet ramps at the malls."

"You took your board to Houston?"

"Don't say it like *that*. You know I suck. You're stronger at that. It's your thing, Wyatt." Joe listened with disgust to the softhearted admiration that had crept into his voice. And it wasn't just admiration, not merely, not simply. It was something more, and that was the problem of his life.

There was silence, and then Wyatt said, "I'm pretty good, aren't I?"

And Joe couldn't help himself. He had to say, "You're actually the best."

■

After he hung up, he scrambled out of bed and into the hall. "Mom," he called. "Mom!" His voice bounced off the mirrors and family photographs on the walls before it soaked into the floor. "Wyatt K.'s going to Houston. Can you zoom me downtown?"

No answer.

He thudded toward the living room and then into the kitchen; ripped open the refrigerator door and peered inside.

His heart had been set on a fried oyster po-boy at the St. Anne Deli. His tongue plumped up with taste memory: crackly, oil-dripping batter; smooth mayo spiked with hot sauce; shredded white lettuce; meaty slices of warm tomato. And then a $1 twenty-ounce draft beer from the bar across the street. Good Friends! It was a rush to walk in there from right off the street when you were hot, you were dragging ass, your skin was filmed over with sweat, your throat was dusty, closing up. You pushed open the saloon doors and—boom! A.C. blasting into the dark, guys shooting pool, ceiling fans swirling, disco tunes boring into your bones. Fuck, boy, some muscle man chances a smile your way. Grab your beer and run or it might turn into more of a night than you expected.

"Mom!" Joe called again, slamming the fridge door shut. "Hey, Mom!"

Still no answer. He listened for a moment, but there were no television or stereo noises. He went to the window above the kitchen sink, looked out into the back yard. The plants were looking rough: burnt edged, droopy from too much rain. The grass, too, looked weak, almost transparently yellow.

And there was Mom, stretched out on one of the stone benches in the center of her little rock garden. A bare foot dangled on the crust of a barren, neatly swept Zen sand plot; an arm covered her eyes; hair hung away from her face, revealing her vulnerable temples; a book rested on her belly. Joe recognized the fake-marble cover; it was one of those lawyer books.

No wonder she fell asleep, he said to himself, turning away from the window.

He spun some notepaper off the roll that hung beside the telephone and wrote a note promising to be home by ten thirty, his curfew.

He changed into a T-shirt and cutoff army pants, rubbed some more deodorant beneath his arms, gargled with Listerine, and then busted out the door. "Hold me, ba-by, drive me, cra-zy," he sang along with the sugary track in his head, crossing the front lawn. He took pains to make deep footprints in the bristly yellow grass. As he reached the curb, a voice called out behind him:

"Joe, what's up?" It was Al Theim.

Looking over his shoulder, Joe said, "What's up with you?"

"I asked you first."

"Yeah?"

"I did."

"Yeah?" They hadn't really talked all summer, not since one night in June when they were fucking around as they always had, wrestling and whatever in Al's bedroom, and Al, laughing, had Joe pinned beneath him, knees holding Joe's arms to the floor, and as if a lifetime's worth of contempt had built up in him, called Joe "the fag of the year." The words had hung there in the chill air of Al's room as if writ large on a banner that fluttered above a stage that Joe was crossing to accept his award.

Now Al walked slowly down the mild slope of his lawn toward Joe's driveway. His breath came with some effort, as if he'd just run wind sprints. He was pulling on a denim baseball shirt that matched his baggy shorts, and a pair of dog tags hung on a length of rawhide around his neck, bouncing against his chest in time with his strides. He was barefoot.

"I wanted to ask you something? I don't ever see you around. What are you doing with yourself? Like, what are you doing this weekend?"

"Well, you can see I'm like taking a walk."

"Yeah."

"Yeah."

"I'm *so* bored, man. I've just been doing shit with my *sister*."

"Oh," Joe said.

"Where you going on your walk? Can I come?" Al stood on one leg, shaking a cramp out of the other. All summer long, he'd been Mr. Buff Cardiovascular Workout. He drilled himself through push-ups and crunches and he walked on his hands. He was building himself into someone new, growing up, leaving behind the fag of the year. At his current frantic pace, he'd soon be hanging with the necky Rods who'd always steered clear of Joe.

"I'm catching the bus," Joe said. "Going to the Quarter."

"Come here," Al said, leaning against the bumper of Mom's car and scratching his back. "I said I'm bored. I want to talk to you man. Let's clear shit up."

Joe looked at his sneakers, shaking his head. "Man, talk to someone else. It makes me feel really stupid. I don't want to talk to you."

"Why can't we just hang? We can like hang. I don't hold any of that against you. I never told anyone anything. Forget *that*. We can, like, hang. Come on."

Joe felt every inch that was between him and Al, and was glad for it. "It doesn't make any sense for us to be friends. I'm not screwing with you, so you should respect me."

Al's eyes were fixed beyond Joe, as if an axman approached.

Joe didn't dare look over his shoulder. "Whatever," Al finally said, pulling back his shoulders so his dog tags swung. He stepped away from the car, heading home. "Let me know when you grow one."

Joe watched him swagger away. "*I've* got a lot to learn, dude, and I admit it," he called, "but I'm not the only one."

Al held up his hand and gave a mincing little backwards wave.

"You suck," Joe whispered.

■

He hiked through his subdivision to Metairie Road, waited twenty minutes for the bus to the Quarter, boarded, had almost fallen asleep when he opened his eyes to see the puny, enticing downtown skyline against the pink clouds. He hopped off the bus at glass-sparkly, boom-boxy, every-kind-of-peoplesy Canal Street. The Mississippi River and the radiant hotels and the fussy gift shops were at one end of Canal. Joe shielded his eyes from the bolts of sunlight that bounced off the surfaces; then he turned and walked in the opposite direction.

Wyatt Who? he asked himself.

Al Who?

■

He caught the streetcar uptown, jumped off at Broadway. Before he knew it, he'd broken into a jog. Six blocks, seven blocks, eight blocks, ten—and why not? The sidewalks were wet, and there were street musicians providing a lazy soundtrack, and the sun-cooked, rain-glistening vines and flowers and leaves emitted a sly fragrance that melted your brain and heart so that all you wanted to do was cry out to someone— anyone who'd tangle up with you—*I love you. Hey, I love you!*

He skidded to a stop in front of So-So's, the music shop that was his and Wyatt's favorite hangout—even though it was also sometimes the favorite of other newbie tenth graders from rival high schools. He busted in the front door and shouted hey to Kel, the studly woman who ran the place.

"Hey, Joe," she said, and then continued with her phone conversation.

"My girl," he said, holding up two fingers in a peace V. He pulled the door shut behind him and walked past her down the narrow aisle of metal shelves and displays of compact discs and cassettes and vinyl.

"I *tried* to read it," she was saying to whomever. "I don't understand what she's getting at. It's the same point in every chapter. I think it's the same argument, which I like *get*, but it's not going to change my mind more than once. Do you know what I'm saying?"

Joe got comfortable in front of a circular turnstile display of World Music cassettes. Some of it he liked. There was a thing called pop-rai, from Algeria, that had gotten his ass shaking at Jazz Fest this past May, and of course he always had a fond ear for salsa music, especially when the singer made you feel like he was lying right beside you on a huge towel on a hot beach.

He looked up from the display at Kel. Fuck if he wasn't totally unfortified against her charms. Kel. Crunchy Kel. She was around thirty or thirty-one, Joe had heard, and she was always looking fly, always hyped on the latest fanzines and demo tapes. She was loose with enthusiasms; she liked to check out your rings, your tattoos, your chokers. She was taller than Joe and even skinnier than he was, had the pointiest elbows that he'd ever touched. She dressed in gutsy little skirts and T-shirts, tan bricklayer's boots. She liked to custommake her clothes, tear off a sleeve and sew it to a different shirt. Her hands were knuckly, like Joe's mom's, and she had long black hair that always smelled like the ocean and was so shiny that you could almost see yourself in it. The girl could give runway.

Mouth agape, Joe drifted to the minidisplay of rap CDs that was propped against Kel's cash register stand. Her muscley white knee peeked from behind it. Today's skirt was tan, and her red T-shirt fit tight on her chest and upper belly, like a tube top.

"That shit hangs real cute on you," he blurted.

She scrunched up her face in thanks.

"Oh, God, I'm sorry; you're on the phone. I should let you finish."

She nodded, and then she let her tongue poke out between her lips and crossed her eyes. She pointed at the phone with the middle finger of her free hand.

Joe smiled. She was having a lame conversation. She had confided in him, made him her ally.

He circled back to the World Music display, lingered for a moment, and then continued to the back of the store. It was dark and cooler back here in the lounge. The furniture was totally easygoing: two floppy red burlap sofas; a brown vinyl beanbag bed; several freestanding green metal ashtrays; and miniature brass temples dangling from chains in which patchouli and lemon-willie incense burned. The tiny, mighty stereo was back here, too, its instrumentation emitting comforting greens and blues. On low volume, Kurt Cobain sang, "choice is yours / don't be late" over hollow red guitar noises.

Joe threw himself onto the closest sofa. The coarse burlap scratched his neck and elbows. He knitted his fingers together behind his neck and closed his eyes.

One night, after the store closed, Kel had shared a joint with him and then had made him try on her olive velvet shirt and pair of red corduroy shorts—just to satisfy her curiosity. She stood right beside him, wearing just her panties and bra, in front of the mirror on the storage-closet door. She made him undo the velvet shirt's bottom two buttons to show off his belly button. "Fabulous hip bones," she murmured. Joe slouched closer to the mirror and gazed into his own eyes. He felt pale with happiness. The clothes looked as if they'd been designed just for him. It was the same pulled-together feeling he'd experienced every now and then when he was at the beach, his hands and feet salt bleached and sand scrubbed to immaculateness.

And then, a little bit drunk and exuding his usual ornate scent, Wyatt K. had snuck up behind Joe and touched his shoulder.

"Doesn't he look . . . ," asked Kel's voice. "You know?" She was somewhere in the room. Anywhere. A corner.

"Yeah," Wy said. He put the flat of his palm on the side of Joe's neck. "If you were a girl, I'd ask you out." His voice was soft. His breath smelled like bananas.

Now Joe rolled onto his other side, pulled the joint from his jeans pocket, and settled into the next Nirvana song. "Work it, Kurt," he said, and lit up. He watched the ember flare and subside as he hit on the joint—three times in quick succession. He wished that Wyatt were here; if he were, Joe thought that his own teeth and tongue might fly out of his mouth and attach to the side of Wy's neck. He wished that he could just see an item of Wyatt's clothing: his wide brown belt, the one with a tarnished buckle, or his stupid Dr. Seuss hat.

"You wanna share?" It was Kel's soft voice, just verging on a giggle. She was standing at the head of the sofa, hovering over him.

"Yeah, girl." He hurried to sit up. "Here, sit down." He patted the cushion next to him.

She fell beside him in a heap; her arms landed at her side and bounced back into the air. "He's just terrible," she said. "But I'm never going to get sick of him."

"Who?" Joe asked.

"Martin. You know my boyfriend, Martin? With the attitude?"

"Oh . . . yeah. I do." He looked at her face in the green-tinted dark. She was making a grimace. "How long have you dated Martin?"

"Too long," she whispered, more to herself than to Joe. She took a hit on the joint and looked up at the ceiling.

"How long's too long?"

"But, you know . . . I feel one way with him and not with anyone else. And that one way is the way I wish I felt all the time. Even if it is impractical. I get so fucking *into* him. When he kisses me—you know how it is when some guys kiss you . . ." She giggled, and then she looked directly into Joe's eyes; she gave him a smile of awful recognition, as if seeing him for the first time. "You know how awful—how totally bottomless—that kind of guy, that kind of kiss . . . God, it can just ruin everything, can't it, Joe?"

7:00 p.m.

Myrtha Murphy Shaw had long ago seen civility and good humor pass from New Orleans public life, but still she was astonished by the hatred that everyone she knew seemed to feel for Rae Schipke. Yes, Rae had used bad judgment. Yes, what Rae had done was wrong. But in any summation of all that had transpired between Rae and the Lady Rampart orphans, surely the orphans came out ahead. They had built their own gilded roost—exploiting their guile and beauty; all that Rae had wanted in return was some affection. Who could begrudge her that?

A pain shot up into Myrtha's back and she doubled over, crying out shrilly, gripping the silk knees of her Beene trousers. With her face tucked against her arm, she sucked in a potent waff of Shalimar, with which she'd drenched herself in the morning, before their first trip over to the courthouse.

The jurors, thank goodness, had remained in disagreement, and Myrtha and Rae had come quickly home. Tonight, the judge had said, we will have a verdict or we will have a mistrial; in the latter case, Rae would disappear, take up residence in Myrtha's Brazilian home.

When the pain had subsided, Myrtha drew herself back to her hobbled height. She looked around doe eyed at the suite in all of its red splendor: musliny wallpaper and satin tapestries and fluttering velvet curtains. She put one foot forward and began lurching daintily, with outward-turned toes, toward the stone wishing well that stood in the center of her room. She had, earlier in the evening, angrily dropped the phone into the still well water.

Now she cocked her head, listening intently. She thought that she heard Rae bustling about in another part of the building. Myrtha cupped her hands around her mouth and let out a holler: "Hel*lo*, Rae! Hel*lo*, dear Rae!"

After she caught her breath, she made it the rest of the way to the wishing well. As she had expected, the phone lay belly-up in the shallow bowl among pennies, nickels, and seashells. She dipped her hand into the water and pulled the phone out. With the help of her other hand, she flicked it open and pushed the TALK button and held the phone to her face.

No dial tone.

Nothing.

Scraps, old girl, she told herself. You've ruined another.

But before she let the phone fall to the floor, she allowed herself a wicked smile and whispered into the mouthpiece, "Count your fingers, count your toes."

7:10 p.m.

The front door exploded open, its bells jingling, and heavy footsteps thudded into the store.

"Hey, bitch, your fun has come." It was White Donna, a disc jockey on WKTT, the alternative-rock station that Joe listened to when he wasn't listening to the rap and soul ballads station.

"*Willkommen*," said Kel. "What's up with you, girl?"

"I'm okay. Sort of."

Joe curled into a sitting position, then pulled himself off the couch. He stood at dopey attention, watching Donna, a spindly, broad-shouldered, tall, self-important chick with her crispy scarlet dreadlock extensions knotted up in tie-dyed rags. She wore a long, clingy black dress and white mules—a good look for her, Joe thought, with her stretch, solid legs.

Kel hung up the phone and leaned across the sales podium

to embrace Donna, as she hadn't when Joe entered. For a moment, he felt as if he'd been jilted, but quickly he drew himself back to swoonish attention and observed the women's every gesture. If he ever wanted a model of seductive, self-assured posture, he had White Donna.

She pulled herself back from Kel, clapped her palms together, and broke into her imitation of Kevin Costner, who, she insisted, had eaten her out when he was in town filming *JFK*. She'd made similar claims about Antonio Banderas, Deion Sanders, and N'dea Davenport. Joe doubted her.

"Just lemme get my nose in the pudding," she rumbled now, sounding nothing like the Kevin Costner that Joe remembered from *Robin Hood*. Her head was cocked to one side; her mouth was open; the silver rings in her nose sparkled. Joe admired the way she kept her hands at her side, didn't make them all fluttery and feminine during her impersonation of a manly coot like Costner.

Letting the performance fall away, Donna asked Kel, "How's tonight for dinner? To Nola? You wanna come with us?"

"Expensive," Kel said with wispy disappointment.

"Yeah? Maybe." Donna propped her elbows on the top of the cash computer. "I wish you'd come. You're so fun to go out to eat with. You always eat so much."

"I know," Kel said dreamily, "but I can't."

"Why?"

"I can't."

"There's something wrong with your life priorities."

"What are you talking about?"

"Oh, my God," Donna said indignantly, "you're on a budget! I thought you were kidding."

Kel's eyes narrowed. "Kinda."

"That's so lame, Kel."

"I'll go to dinner," Joe called from the dark hollow of the lounge.

"Joe!" Donna said. "What's up, boy?"

He pushed himself toward her, past the bins of CDs and cassettes, past the hanging racks of band T-shirts; he kept his bleary gaze fixed on her chin. When he was within a yard of her, he said, "I'll go out to dinner with you."

"My boyfriend's going, too." She turned her face sideways and grinned, trying to meet his eyes. Her cheek and chin were bathed with weak dusty evening sun. "Is that cool with you?"

"Yeah—wait, you still dating Black Chris?"

"Well . . ."

"He's good for you?"

"Yeah?"

"Oh, fuck," Kel said sweetly, "Now I wish I could go, too. It sounds fun. Mommy, Daddy, and Joe."

"I'll buy you dinner," Joe said, shifting his eyes hopefully. He had his own credit card. He had his own bank account. His daddy had taught him how to make a budget and how to ignore it when the occasion was right.

"I really can't, sooka. I'm not supposed to go to the Quarter for a few weeks."

"Huh," Joe said.

Donna covered her eyes with one buffed hand. "I can't even believe this shit. What's wrong with the Quarter? What is it now? Next thing, you'll say you're moving to San Francisco. Why does everyone want to leave. Go someplace *better.* What's better about San Francisco?"

"Nothing?" Joe offered.

Kel shuddered. "Ooooh. I'm not moving. If I do, it's maybe to Houston. Not to San Fran."

Donna dropped her hand from her face. "Good."

"Houston's cool," Joe said. "Wyatt K.'s there this weekend."

"It's okay," Kel said. "Houston will do. In a pinch. Don't get carried away with your love of Houston. I could tell you about Houston if you really wanted to know."

"But how come you can't go to the Quarter?"

"Let's just say . . ." She held her hands in front of her as if displaying grapefruit.

"Don't tell this boy your dirty shit." Donna laughed and then put her arm around Joe's shoulder. "All your nasty stories to this poor boy. *You.*"

Joe tried to nestle closer to her so that her scent would linger on his T-shirt. "I would like to hear some dirty stories."

"Come over here," she said, pulling him toward the tall metal New Release display, looking past his eyes at Kel. "I want you to tell me some songs to play tomorrow. I'm sick of the songs I've got, and the competition's gunnin' for me."

■

Joe was sitting on the window ledge beside the front door, watching the dimming street and the twirling leaves of gnarled-limb trees, when a Jeep full of buzzhead shirtless guys pulled into the gravelly driveway that ran beside the store and skidded to a stop. In jubilant unison, the boys raised their husky arms over their heads. Bubbles of rhyme flew out of their stereo speakers; Joe could hear it inside the store: sly, clear-voiced Ladybug chanting, "Nickel bag, a nickel bag . . ."

"It's them," Kel said, looking over her shoulder out the window. She was taking inventory of the indie label cassettes. "Wow, they showed up."

"Who are they?" Joe asked.

"Some of the orphans. Rad orphans." She broke into a high, childish voice: "All we ever get is gru-el." She pulled herself away from the cassettes and went back to the sales podium, found the remote control wand, and pointed it toward the back of the store; the keyboards and cymbals of a bullshit new dance-music group swelled to fill every corner. It wasn't the good kind of disco, whose beats made Joe's hidden emotions apparent to him; it was a dull, ballady song tricked up with a bunch of swirls and kabooms.

White Donna, at sonic ground zero in the lounge, shook her dreads, wiggled her arms at the shoulder, and on every fourth beat clapped her hands satirically.

"I don't know if I believe the orphans," Kel blurted over the music. "You never know who's lying these days." She pressed her face beside Joe's, watching out the window. "Those guys have a pretty burly aspect to their chests and arms. You wouldn't think they could get abused—you know?"

"They're in their prime, that's for sure. Whatever." Joe felt a blackness approaching his peripheral vision, like a premonition that he was about to lose consciousness: he thought for a moment that maybe his desire for the boys in the Jeep had gushed out of his brain and heart, bounced off the window, and come back on him with a vengeance. He bit down on the inside of his cheek. "They're from that orphanage? Really? Why are they here?"

"I know some of those guys."

"Which ones?"

"Him and him," Kel said, putting her finger to the glass, pointing.

"That's a help."

"Yeah. You'll meet them if you'd like. Do you want to meet them?"

"It's just weird." Joe continued to watch, transfixed by their fucking around. Kel leaned against him, her chest folding against his shoulder.

After a while, she asked, "Why?"

"Nothing."

"Oh."

"I'm gonna go check them out." Joe unhooked her arm from around his waist and started away from her.

"They're kind of rough. Be careful."

"Please, queen." Joe swung the door outward, paused, and stepped onto the front porch. Clicking the door shut behind him, he self-consciously turned toward the Jeep, from which jazzy beats continued to flow: the rapper Butterfly singing, "Babies man, we're just babies, man . . ."

"What's up?" Joe called. His voice was swallowed up in the stereo's fat, squiggly samples, so he shouted out again to the four guys. They were all dark skinned, reddish brown, with ropey arms and strong necks and baldish round skulls.

The music went silent; after a moment of crackling feedback, the boy who was driving shouted into a handheld microphone, and his voice thundered out of the heavy speakers: "Hello, friend! Justice for the Lady Rampart orphans!" His voice was woody and deep; it chopped syllables short.

Joe's temples and armpits and the backs of his knees tingled with perspiration. "Whoa," he said. "Is that your *slo*gan?"

"Yup," the voice bellowed.

"I guess it's direct." Joe didn't recognize the four guys, but that didn't surprise him: all over town, you'd run into people you'd never seen before, people whose faces and bodies and demeanors were so arresting that you couldn't believe the town would contain them. But these boys—especially the driver with the scruffy chin stubble and bulky shoulders. If these were some of the famous orphans, why hadn't they been on TV? Joe'd watched a lot of the coverage, looking for a guy he knew who was serving on the jury.

"You do us a favor, man?" asked the one in the front passenger seat. He was maybe too buff—or maybe not; there was cute blond hair on his craggy, sunburned chest and belly.

"What?"

"Where's Kel?" the driver said, this time without the microphone. "She told us we could hang one of our banners here."

"Kel's inside." He considered backing against the front door, knocking on the glass to get her attention, but decided not to. "She told me to come out and help you guys."

"Donna said she was gonna be here," said the blond.

"All right," said the driver. "Donna. What's up with Donna lately?"

"She's helpin' Kel," Joe said. "She's in a bad mood."

"You wanna help us?" The driver's voice hung right beside Joe's ears; it had traveled across the front porch, snuck up on him, and now it was lingering.

Joe found himself loping down the stairs, off the porch. Each step closer to the side of the Jeep made the driver's appearance more radiant. Joe stumbled a few final steps and wrapped his hand around the side-view mirror. "Hey," he said.

"You're going to help us?"

"Yeah," Joe said. "Let's get it on. Let's hang this banner."

"Look who's down with us," said one of the two boys in the backseat. They were twins, with identical eyebrows, foreheads, and mouths.

"Righteous," said the first boy's twin, whose nose and voice were bigger than his brother's.

"He's cool. I can tell." The driver started to get up, the muscles in his belly tightening. He snatched a folded-up sheet off his seat; then he leaned over the edge of the Jeep, locked his knees, put his free hand on Joe's shoulder, and dumped himself over the door. As he landed, the side of his chest and belly pressed against the length of Joe's arm. The back of Joe's neck tingled.

"Here." He handed Joe two corners of a sheet and then, holding two corners himself, backed away so that it opened. The words ORPHANS and VICTORY, in blocky red Magic Marker, were poorly centered but, Joe thought, kind of compelling. "Let's hang it across the front window. When we win this trial, we're going to have some serious independence, dude, and you can say you helped out. You'll have, you know, a place in our hearts."

"Okay."

They thudded up the stairs to the front porch. "We can hang it from that spandrel," the boy said, pointing at the top of the window. "Looks like somebody tore the wood off; we can use those nails sticking out of the brick."

"Those?" Joe pointed.

"Yup."

"I better go get a ladder."

"No time, bud. No time to waste. I'll hoist ya." He twisted his neck; it was peeling, and there was a dirt handprint across his Adam's apple. He noticed Joe watching him and laughed. "We just came from downtown. Got interviewed for the news tonight. They got us to horse around for the cameras."

"Fuck," Joe said.

"My name's Welk."

"I'm Joe Keith."

"You ready to hang this banner?" He handed Joe his corners of the sheet, bent at his knees, and locked his fingers to make his hands into a step.

"You're not gonna drop me?"

"No."

"You're sure."

He reached across the space between them and with his finger drew an *X* on Joe's chest. "Never. Besides, what do you weigh—ninety-five?"

"Bullshit." Joe lifted his left foot up into the hand step. "Ready," he said, and he was floating up into the air. He grabbed Welk's shoulder, but the shock of touching him made Joe let go. He put his free hand on the side of the house and tried to break the corner of the sheet over a nail. "Can you move me a little to the right?" he asked Welk.

"Done."

Joe lurched sideways and felt Welk move his chest and stomach closer to him—against the backs of Joe's legs—for balance.

When Joe was done, Welk lowered him to the ground but kept his palm flat against Joe's lower back. One of Welk's fingers slipped beneath the waistband of Joe's boxer shorts and then pulled back out.

The Jeep horn beeped.

As Joe turned around, Welk's hand slid around the side of his T-shirt. "Thanks, man," Welk said, thick voiced.

"Yeah."

"I gotta run." Welk's eyes were drifting shut.

"Yeah—well, are you in high school? How old are you?"

Eyes flew open. "Not any more. I'm emancipated. I'm nineteen. I go to, um, Tulane. Sophomore. How old are you?"

"Sixteen."

"I can play that."

Joe closed his eyes and let his heart bust around inside his ribs. Then he went for it. "You wanna hook up later, get a beer?"

Welk drew his head back in an exaggerated double take. "Boy!"

"Well?"

"Could be."

"Do you go to Tipitina's ever? Lafitte's ever? You ever go to Oz?"

"I might."

"Look, I don't mean to sound all grindy and eager," Joe said, "but . . . well, do you wanna meet up later? It would be cool to talk to you about the trial and shit. I know someone on the jury."

"No way."

"Way."

Welk reached his hand across the space between them and flicked a wasp from Joe's shoulder; it buzzed its way to the front door, rested on a window. "How'd I just end up meeting you? How'd that happen?" He looked up at the sky; with his chin still pointing up, he glanced at Joe out of the corner of his eye.

The Jeep horn beeped again, twice.

"Yeah, I wanna meet up," Welk said. He brought his face back to its normal position; his mouth and eyes were serious. "Absolutely."

"Oz? Midnight?"

The horn went longer.

"I'll be there from eleven on," Welk said.

"Cool." Joe held out his hand; they shook.

"Tonight."

"Later." Joe watched Welk saunter toward the Jeep. Man with a mission, he said to himself.

The other orphans stood in their seats, saluting as the Jeep pulled out of the driveway. They stood with their feet apart, shoulders squared. Welk gunned the Jeep engine and settled back, letting one arm hang out the side.

When they were gone, the street was quiet. All of the trees

and windowy house facades and curbside cars were just sitting there, heating up beneath the ragged, black, boiling sky. Joe watched it all.

.

Back inside, he walked slowly toward the rear of the store, where Kel and Donna were sharing a cigarette. He could smell it burning and see its red ember floating in the dark lounge.

"Hey," he called out.

"Hey."

"Who dat?"

"Us."

"Doh!" He lingered just on the threshold of the lounge, peering in at the women, who lay side by side on the beanbag. On the stereo, a guitar was making hollow, orange noises over a steady drumbeat.

"What's going on?" asked Donna. "How're those orphans?"

"One of them's the shit," Joe said. "Welk? And I think he's into me."

"Into *you?*"

Kel groaned. "Our boy's growing up. Joe, you're making me feel old."

"Wait, wait," Joe said. "Don't judge me. I have a question for you guys."

"Us? We tired."

"Don't be all wretched," Donna said. "Leave it to us nasty wenches to be all wretched." She dropped her chin onto Kel's shoulder.

"You guys," Joe asked, "do you think anybody really got abused?"

"I'm telling you, it's supposed to have been the little kids at the home. Not these guys."

Joe shuffled toward the beanbag. "I don't know what to think about them as a group. I guess I don't even give a fuck—about them as a group. If I'm going to be honest."

"So there are some sparks flying betwixt you and Welk?" Kel said.

"You know, he calls me a lot," Donna said. "How weird is that? Guys don't call me. When I get past the opening conversation, I get into some good shit with Welk. Like, sometimes I don't want to get off the phone. Which for me is unusual."

"You're not being honest. You're so different on the phone. Kind of sweet, kind of moral." Kel rubbed the back of her hand down Donna's neck.

"I like when you talk nice about me. It's so weird. I'm just getting a shiver. My defenses are falling."

"I'm nice to you a lot of the time. Most of the time."

Donna said, "I know. I guess I'm confusing you with my boyfriend, or my mother."

"Are you guys going to talk to me or not?" Joe asked. "Are you just going to ignore me? Be all adult and shit?"

"But back to you a minute, Joe." Kel sighed. "I get a good feeling from Welk. And I think that he is totally gay. I think that's what I've heard. I don't know very much about his history or anything."

"Neither do I," Donna said.

"That's amazing," Joe said, and pressed his palms to his heart. "I'm supposed to hang with him later." He dropped to his knees beside the girls. "Can I have a drag?" Kel handed him the cigarette, from which he inhaled deeply. Blowing smoke, he said, "I am head over heels. If I could just make something happen, some sort of love life, then I think I could concentrate on the rest of my life. I mean, I kind of wanna develop into a complete person."

Chunky drums joined the orange guitars on the music that billowed from the stereo.

"Well," said Donna, "that's good."

"We want that for you," Kel said. Then, in a sad voice, she added, "I wonder if there's any hope for me."

"Don't," Joe said, his voice going higher. "Don't make me be the one to offer advice. That's totally not fair."

"Um . . ."

"I'm serious."

"I can hear that in your voice."

"Well, then don't. I want you to show me the ropes. *Fuck.* What do I know?"

"You *don't* know very much, do you?" Donna asked.

"No, I don't. I'm not even trying to pretend like I do."

Donna rolled out of the beanbag's lap and pushed herself into a standing position. "If you want advice, you're gonna have to think of specific questions. I'm sorry, but I can't just, like, extemporaneously settle your heart. But ask me a question."

"Okay." He settled into the warm spot where Donna had been lying, and dropped his head into the fragrant crook of Kel's elbow.

"Hey, sweetie," Kel said. She kissed the back of his neck.

"Hey, Kel." His shoulder was pressed against her rib cage; as she breathed, her side rubbed against him.

"So ask me a question," Donna said; she'd disappeared in the dark next to the stereo. "I'm willing to put some heart into this one. Take your opportunity."

"Okay. Okay, here's a question."

"Shoot."

Joe spoke softly into the beanbag chair. "I'm not unreasonable. I know that I'm maybe going to have to meet and deal with all different people before I meet someone who's like the right person for me. I totally accept that."

"Good start," Kel said.

"So what I want to know is how thick of a skin I have to grow. Like, how hard is it to keep connecting and tearing away from people—in a romantic context, I mean, 'cause I really don't know, in that way?"

"What do you think?" Kel said, almost impatiently. "You have instincts. You've had some experience in this love thing. We've talked about certain people, certain kisses."

After a while, over the stereo's hissing synthesizers and echoing drumbeats, Joe said, "See, I'd guess you'd need to have maybe medium skin, maybe alligator, 'cause you wouldn't want to be too tough. Wouldn't it be a turnoff, if you were too tough?"

"My advice," Donna said from her dark corner, "is to go to one extreme or the other. Have no skin or have metal armor. But let me tell you something about metal armor. It gets a shitty rap. You can be thinking and feeling as genuinely as anyone else and still have metal armor. You can love somebody with four or five hearts. You totally can. And you can still have the metal armor, protecting you, preventing you from getting unduly messed with. You don't have to show every little piece of yourself. And I'm saying this as someone who does *not* have the armor herself. Who has like never had the armor. Who, for herself, does not want the armor. I know a lot of people say they can take it; they can take whatever heartache gets ladled on top of them. A lot of them are liars. But I'm not. I've been to hell and back, have I not?"

"You have," Kel said.

"Yeah, you totally have," Joe said.

"I've put my righteous love and devotion right out there in the open, and it's been stomped on, and I'm still here. For me, it's the noble route. For you . . . ?"

Kel giggled. "Oh," she said, "I wish we were dykes, Donna. That's how much I'm in love with you."

Joe, his heart constricted with jealousy, closed his eyes and sighed.

7:50 p.m.

Over the course of the summer, Al Theim had put away his Sega and his chemistry set, his medieval role-playing games, his comics, major league pennants, and the tattered, dart-holed poster of past Saints quarterback Bobby Hebert, who'd chumped the team to join the Falcons. Al and his sister had scraped off the Chincoteague wallpaper and painted the walls white. Now the bedroom reflected his resolve to begin anew, to forge unintimidated through his final two years of school at Country Day, where, previously, he'd always been part of the loosey-goosey Joe Keith crowd. The room was austere, just bed, dresser, desk, Macintosh, a wall of mirror tiles, a boom box that his brother, who'd just moved to Durham, North Carolina, for college, had passed down to him.

Al was in position on the hardwood floor, pumping out

push-ups and singing along with a song he'd been turning on to all summer—a wiggly little guitar line, some candy-girl strings, fussy cymbals, and that low-down piss-ignorance coming out of Barry White's mouth. Joe Keith had introduced him to Mr. White's fables, and for that Al would be forever grateful; this music was about as close to lovemaking as Al had gotten all summer. Enough said.

Al had goals for himself, and the most important was an end to his virginity, but first he had to make himself presentable. So far, since beginning this regimen, he'd put on what—ten pounds? That was a shy, scrimpy number. His chest was no longer concave and his legs weren't still just *sticks*, but Al wanted veins, and peaks, and density, and distortion. He wasn't going to be satisfied until he was the most Mike Tysonish Al Theim that he could be, and dis*tress* to those who sweated the old Al.

"Hooh!" he groaned, attempting to one-arm the twenty-first push-up; he had a wobble on the extension, so he let the other arm help on the downward trip.

Twenty-two.

Twenty-three.

Twenty-four.

The innermost tissue of his chest burned, and his upper arms were heavy, but he had no soreness in his shoulder sockets or the machinery of his elbows. Good-bye to those timid half answers, good-bye to averted eyes, good-bye to shuffling demeanor.

Al toughed out five last reps and dropped his chest to the floor. It was time for abdominal crunches, the dullest part of any deadly dude's daily routine. As he flipped onto his back and crossed his arms over his chest for the first set of forty, the tape ended and the machine switched automatically to the radio. It was an all-talk station, and many sorts of ill human species were suddenly filling up Al's room with their voices.

Al, with a sort of disingenuously furtive glance, checked out his arm muscles as he crunched. Looking fine; looking thicker. It would be so dicky when he could actually wear a T-shirt and sort of *expose* his pipes. Girlies'd be so susceptible, as they weren't to the spindly twigs that Joe Keith carried on him.

A lady caller spoke sharply to the radio host: "It could have been *me!* Ten thirty at night! It could have been anyone I know; we have all been in the Quarter ten thirty at night—"

Then she was interrupted by a different lady's more professional voice: "This is Gladys Durr Smith with a WRYC news break. Deliberations continue in the civil trial of Myrtha Shaw Charity Trust executive Rae Schipke. The judge announced at noon today that he had received a note from the jury indicating that a verdict was possible by midnight; if the jury is unable to break its five-day impasse, the judge will declare a mistrial. Schipke, thirty-seven, a Dallas native, is alleged to have sexually abused two young boys she befriended from a French Quarter orphanage. More news at the top of the hour. Back to Talk Talk and Jim Woodside."

Al, his belly burning, was lost in the splendor of the news reader's voice. He wanted her to come pouring out of the speakers and kiss him.

Kiss me, he thought. Come kiss me. He hadn't had a kiss since his friendship with Joe Keith ended, but he figured he'd be better off waiting for a girl; making do, fucking around with a guy, and especially with a guy who he'd thought was his best friend, had resulted in all sorts of shitty fallout. He could have handled it all with a lot more finesse.

It had never occurred to Al, never ever, not for one moment of the last four years, that Joe would actually fall in love with him. What kind of signal wreck could have caused such a massive delusion? They had, for four years, like *wrestled*, and talked late at night on the phone or in person, out in the back yard; they'd gotten dressed in front of each other, and sort of pretending that one of them was the guy and the other was a girl, they had put their hands places that Al guessed they shouldn't have; and, in the same spirit, they'd whispered endearments, and kissed on the other's dry lips. But that was just fucking around; it wasn't as Joe had derailed himself into *thinking*, which was bad enough, and then on that stupid night earlier this summer, actually coming out and *saying*, with a katrillion watts of seriousness. It wasn't that at all.

■

When Al finished his last crunch, he picked up the *Time* that lay beside him on the floor and paged through it while at the same time he listened to a radio interview with a man named Marcus Damico who'd dropped out of high school to work as a professional fireworks lighter. Damico had a wussy voice, but it hadn't stopped him from acting just as he pleased, from moving city to city, to wherever he pleased, and taking charge of all the celebrations that required fireworks. Al guessed that somebody had to set the things off.

His stomach bleated pathetically. It was time for another one of his sickening high-protein, low-fat shakes. Al could hear the blender; he could taste the wheaty chocolate. What he truly craved was a forbidden slice of sausage pizza, left over in the fridge downstairs. But there was no way to sneak down there for shakes or pizza; his sister and her sickly, milky-fingered, blue-toothed friend Angela Bell were playing Risk at the kitchen table. Angela had taken a liking to him and needed no excuse to pinch his belly or triceps and exclaim over his developing physique.

Time was not exactly the tough reading that Al had once considered it; the articles were shorter than anything he was assigned at school. You couldn't exactly linger over it, even if you were at the same time listening to Marcus Damico drone on about the mystery and danger of making fireworks. He laid it beside him with a low belch.

8 : 0 0 p . m .

Joe sat cross-legged on the cement streetcar stop at the intersection of St. Charles and Broadway, wondering what the night would bring. Sometimes you had to apprehend the whole coming stretch—ask yourself what you wanted from the hours; otherwise, like when you just hung out, minute tumbling upon minute, expecting the best, nothing much happened. Joe had had such nights. Leaky disappointments. Tonight he wanted commotion.

Cars slipped past him. The high leaves of spruce and walnut trees swayed in the fitful breeze. In the distance, the single headlight of the streetcar approached. He was lucky to be here, in this city, full of hope.

You could be all empty and shit, he thought; you could feel like nothing here in New Orleans. Blank, blank, blank. That could be your real personality, but your skin and your soul and whatever else made up you, all of the raw materials, would absorb the city. The city did the work for you; when you didn't feel like being anything, you didn't have to: you were just somebody who lives in New Orleans. Joe thought that's why his daddy had liked the city. Daddy had always wanted to be more than he was, to make a good biography: he'd moved Joe and Joe's mom from Pennsylvania to Florida to Alabama, changing jobs from hospital orderly to handyman to waiter, and then, when he finally settled here in New Orleans, his life fell in place: he managed a big restaurant, met TV stars and blues guitarists, politicians, the casino players. Not that they remembered him when he died. Daddy would have been pissed, Joe thought, at the low turnout to his funeral.

Whatever. Tonight there were stars down low to the sky, inky blue with spills of tomato red in the clouds, and there were the big lighted houses on the Avenue, and there were the front porches of the smaller houses on the side streets. If Joe could live anywhere in the city, it would be on such a stretch of homes. He was drawn to the dark first-floor windows and the compact pillars and the peeling shutters veiled by husky, knotted vines and splayed tree trunks; and to the dark wet lairs of lawn between the houses, and the hanging lanterns pitching their light into the wind so that it might drift into the night. Maybe tonight he would have been content to sit on a front porch with a magazine and a glass of iced tea. Stretched. Reclined. Listening to the muted noises around him.

Maybe nothing as exciting as meeting Welk would happen later tonight. He'd go eat dinner with White Donna, have some beers. There was maybe a chance that he'd see Welk, but he couldn't count on it. Fuck if that orphans' trial would just hurry up and end soon. It kept fucking up his love life.

For instance, he'd set up a date with the guy he'd met at his mom's gym—Seth, who was a juror in the trial, sequestered for the duration. The weeks had passed quickly since then. Joe had been engrossed in fantasies about the guy, but now there was Welk, who already seemed like something more. Welk was closer to his age, and more intense, funkier. There had been some electricity between them, Joe thought. He wasn't just fooling himself.

But still. Seth, man . . .

Joe had kept seeing the dude, for almost a year, at the New Orleans Athletic Center on Rampart, the moldering block at the Canal Street edge of the Quarter. Watching him. Trying to be nonchalant.

Then, like a month ago . . . It was after nine, so the place was empty. Mom was downstairs in the Nautilus room. Sweet Barry White song shimmering out of the speakers in the spanky, tropical-steamy, white-tile natatorium. That big-ass voice on top of strings and buckets of rhythm. And there's Joe wearing swim trunks he'd made by cutting off some coal-and-red-plaid Stussy slacks; taking long, long, keep-on-truckin' strides around the perimeter of the pool, a bit off balance, snapping his fingers in time to the Barry White backup chicks. *Splish, splish, splash* went Joe's feet in the warm overspill trough of the pool.

He threw his hands over his head and jumped to tap the bottom of a hanging plastic planter; jumped up again, shouting "gimme!" and grabbed a handful of leaves that toppled over the planter's brim. Three pieces of leaf came off in his fist.

"Whatcha up to?" shouted Seth over the music. He'd just busted out of the locker room, which was near Joe's end of the pool but on the opposite side of the water. He was wrapped in a small white towel, hair dripping from the shower, beads of water inching down the front of his chest. When he made eye contact with Joe, he stopped in midstep and grinned.

"*Nada,*" Joe answered faintly, and kept walking. He'd talked to Seth just a few times, when they were side by side on the Lifecycles or the leg machines or soaping up in the big shower room—the last had been kind of embarrassing: steam rising from the tile floor, Seth so cute and friendly and freckly, his dick flopping in his hands as he lathered.

"I'm not much of a dancer," Seth called across the water. He was clapping his hands on the count of three, submitting to the rhythm. His knees shot up to his waist and his arms pumped like a relay runner's.

No, Joe thought, not much of a dancer. But they were sweet fucking buff muscles on those arms. Joe splashed toward the far wall of the pool, and Seth, from the opposite side, made his way there, too. "You're gonna lose your towel," Joe said, "or throw your back out."

"Nah, I'm coordinated. It's all mental. I can hold this towel around my waist by sheer force of will."

"That's a cool trick."

Barry White grunted over some diaphonous strings and low-rustling drums.

They stood facing each other now, a few yards apart at the deep end.

Seth dropped from the dry cement into the overspill trough and slid up against him. "It's not a trick." He stood on the backs of his feet; the muscles above his knees bulged and shifted; their structure and functional, inevitable movement reminded Joe of the models of tectonic plates that his geology teacher kept on her desk.

When he looked up from the legs, he saw that Seth was grinning. "Cocky sumbitch," Joe said in a joking voice. He had floated a foot or two into the air; his stomach was still catching up. The way Seth was looking at him was different than when they were in the shower. It was the look that studly guys on TV gave their girlfriends after learning the girlfriend was pregnant. It was sickening and irresistible and it had its own smell. Joe couldn't look away. He touched his belly.

Seth's eyes were the color of walnut shells. His nose was blunt and spread across his face. He was a half foot taller than Joe, and he smelled of dandruff shampoo and aloe lotion. Lumps of the lotion remained on his shoulders and stomach. Before he knew what he was doing, Joe reached out to smooth a knot of the goo into Seth's shoulder. He held his hand on the shoulder cap for a moment and then drew it back and wiped it across his own stomach.

Seth didn't say anything for a while; he just stared at Joe's hand. Then he said, "That felt really good. You wanna rub these?" He pointed to a white squiggle on his chest, near the hollow at the bottom of his neck; as his wrist turned, his biceps plumped into an apple.

Joe tossed himself into the pool. He pulled his way to the bottom, pressed his belly to the tile, and then floated to the surface. He kept his eyes blared open in the burning water.

When he was out of breath, he lifted his head and bobbed to the side. He hooked his armpits over the apron, dangled his hands and forearms into the overspill trough. The water *lap lap lap*ped along the edge.

Seth was gone.

"Damn," Joe said. He looked around the pool area: hanging plants, tile walls, the glazed windows that overlooked the service entrance at the back of the building. He ran his gaze along the far tile wall, to the point where the symmetry of the squares disappeared among the leaves of two potted trees that stood sentry before a dark storage recess. And there was Seth's face, wreathed in green.

"Hey," Joe called, pushing himself out of the pool, knees bumping against the slippy tile. "What you doing over there?"

Seth made a sharp whistle.

"What?" Joe said, and then he realized that his trunks had slid low on his hips. He pulled them up as he plopped across the floor; even though the room was humid and warm, goose pimples rose on his legs and arms and stomach.

Seth slipped into the dark alcove.

When Joe got there, he saw that it was just big enough to hold a refrigerator. He stopped on the pool side of the trees. "What's going on?" he whispered.

"I want to show you something," Seth whispered back.

"What if someone sees us?"

Seth laughed. "If you just come in here right now, then there's less of a chance."

"I'm here," Joe said, stepping past the tree line. Two steps, and his belly was against the towel around Seth's waist.

"Hey, Joe," Seth said softly.

Just the sound of Seth's voice in the dark made Joe feel all muzzy headed. His wet dick was getting hard.

Seth's hands were behind his back. "What's your deal?" he asked.

Joe didn't answer.

"Can I touch your face?" Seth asked.

What for, Joe thought, *my stupid face*; but he said, "I don't care."

And, like that, Seth's big hand was touching the side of Joe's neck, and then the fingertips were drumming his cheek.

"Can I kiss you?" Seth asked.

"That would be cool. Can I kiss you?"

Seth's throat rumbled as his hand squeezed the back of

Joe's head, and they were all of a sudden kissing: Joe's tongue along the underside of Seth's lips, inside his cheeks; and Seth's tongue filled up Joe's mouth, and his whole body shook, and his heart beat so loudly that Joe could feel it against his own skin.

Abruptly, Seth stopped. "Fuck," he panted. "Would you wanna do something with me—in a couple weeks—fuck!—a month, a month; I'm starting jury duty next Tuesday. Things are gonna be crazy."

"Yeah," Joe said.

Seth bent down to snatch his towel off the floor. "Okay. You go out first. Make sure the coast's clear."

Joe's mind's eye had sunk lower—through his face, throat, chest, stomach, down into his dick. He whispered, "But we could do a little more back here, maybe." He tried to catch his breath, stood there huffing, watching Seth fasten the towel. "I'm afraid I'm going to go home—me, just me, alone with my mom—and what if we die in the car or something and I never get a chance . . ." The sound of his breath was filling up his ears. "This is more than I thought was ever going to happen on just a fucking Tuesday night . . . I mean . . ."

Seth made a soothing noise in his throat. He was already cloaking himself around Joe; his hands went down the back of Joe's bathing suit, pulling it down. "We got some time," he said. "I can always find time."

Joe's hands flopped across the front of Seth's body. It was full of contrasts—hairy, smooth, tight, bulky, wet—and in his sickening nervousness Joe found himself groping Seth kind of passionlessly, as if he had no desire for him at all. But, fuck, that wasn't true. From a distance, like when he watched Seth lift weights or talk to the girl beside him on the stair machines, Joe time after time experienced internal instantaneous carnal transmogrifications; the backs of his eyes and the canals of his ears and the bone at the base of his spine had all burned in unison.

Joe thought that making out had always gone pretty easily for him. It was something he loved to do. Girls or boys, just lie down somewhere and kiss. At parties, in back yards, at school. But he had never really kissed around with anyone older than him—experienced and filled out and dead set on going from kiss to grope to pin to penetration.

"This isn't the right place, is it?" Seth said, separating from him.

"Maybe not."

"Well, is it or isn't it?"

"I guess not."

"No, boy. Yes or no. You wanna do—"

"No. Not here."

Seth was already leaning over, picking his towel and Joe's bathing suit up off the floor. "Here," he said, "step into them."

Joe took them out of his hand. "I can get myself dressed, sunshine."

Seth's voice was suddenly distant. "I'll call you when this trial is finished, how's that?" He wrapped the towel around his waist.

"That rocks."

"Okay, we'll just walk out there like nothing. No one's out there."

Joe threw his hearing outside of the immediate space. All that he could hear was the continued moaning of Barry White over the most sticky-sweet, high-tension strings.

As Seth stepped past the potted trees out into the bright lights, Joe's veins filled up with relief and he could breathe, and his hands and feet began to tingle as if they'd been asleep.

He leaned back against the wall, closing his eyes, listening to Barry White murmur.

He was feeling almost normal, ready to go downstairs and find his mom, when a voice boomed from the other side of the trees—"But what have you been *up* to?"—and then a woman's face pushed through the leaves and she shouted, "But I want to meet him! Seth, I want to meet him."

A pretty, pale face, hair pulled back, leaves hanging below her ears. Big smile. The woman's arms extended toward him like an octopus's or a starfish's. "Seth," she said, "who's your little friend? What's his name?"

Joe's balls had drawn up into his belly. He was light headed, breathing too quickly.

"Rae . . ." It was Seth's voice, irritated.

The woman stepped over the trees and into the alcove. She wore a one-piece that showed off her rack. She extended her hand. "Hi, I'm Rae Schipke."

"Joe," he said, and held out his hand; as he shook with the woman, he slid past her along the wall and out into the bright natatorium. His feet peeled along the tile floor. He was just in time to see Seth's backside disappear between the swinging doors of the locker room.

He looked reproachfully over his shoulder in the direction of the woman, caught her dead gaze as she climbed out of the alcove, held it for a moment before jogging the length of the pool and busting through the doors after Seth. Two skinny bodybuilders were standing just inside the room, at the head of an empty row of redwood lockers. A boom box at their feet was bellowing the play-by-play of a baseball game; the men grimaced as a player hit a pop fly. Joe passed them and looked down the next two rows of lockers. As he continued to the final row, he heard a loud cough and felt a hand on his shoulder. He spun around to face Seth, who handed him a business card.

"Here's my numbers," Seth said. "Keep an eye on the TV. Call me when you see that the trial's over. I'm lookin' forward to it."

■

The streetcar wheezed to a stop and its door folded open. Joe climbed inside the brightly lighted car, slid his dollar into the receptacle as the driver closed the door and they began moving.

He swayed down the aisle, took a seat in the back, and settled against the side of the car, pressing his cheek against the window. The bald guy in the seat in front of him was sweating as if he'd just run an ironman. Across the aisle, and a seat farther front, two nuns were turned around, smiling at Joe with the openness of children.

"Good evening," he said.

"Hello," the nuns said at the same time.

Two bearded Tulane chippies were in the seat behind him. He was sitting on top of their conversation. "I don't know," said one guy, with a pipsqueaky voice. "There's a lot of them who aren't in a hurry to find a job. Me, I'm gonna get a job. They're interviewing B.E.E. to start at thirty-five up north at Medtronic. I tried to get an interview, but they don't want Mechanical E."

"I interviewed with them," said the other guy, whose words rushed together. "Within five years, so they say, you're making eighty. I didn't get called for the second round of interviews."

"I owe twenty-four thousand in student loans? I should be, like, furiously searching for a fifty-thousand dollar job?"

"Dude, you owe that much?"

The guy in front of Joe turned around in his seat and scowled back at the Tulane guys. Then he looked Joe straight in the face with eyes that were the green of watermelon shell. His lips were plump and wet.

" 'Sup?" he asked.

"What's up," Joe said.

"Hi." He perched his forearm on the top of the seat back and continued to stare at Joe. "Do I know you?"

"Do you think you do?"

"I think maybe I do. I've acquired knowledge. I'm seeing life. I'm seeing . . . Your old men shall see dreams and your young men shall see visions. It's scary because I have visions. Are you with me?"

"I can't help you out, hoss. I don't recognize you."

Joe settled back into the comforting patter of nebbishy Tulane students on their way to good jobs; it was cool to take a detour into their reasonable, mellow world for a little while. They weren't visionaries.

"I wore brown shoes," the squeaky-voiced guy was saying. "Do you think that was appropriate?"

"Well . . . ," said his friend.

No, Joe thought to himself, picturing loafers with tassels.

The streetcar rumbled beneath the highway overpass and stopped at a traffic light; the door opened and new passengers began climbing aboard. The wet breeze had picked up. It drew the tree branches higher, but they didn't sway; the leaves shook within a tight circumference, as if reverberating from a silent aftershock. Hurricane season, Joe remembered. The wheels began to grind along the track. He pressed his forehead against the shaking window, looking out; the sky had grown lighter with clouds, as if night weren't here. Let the rain hold off for another twenty minutes, he said to himself. A half hour.

He turned away from the window and bent down to retie his sneakers; the laces were so frayed they barely held a knot. Resting his chin on his knee, he wondered why he was even going out to dinner. Why didn't he just hang on Decatur Street, talk to other kids? What was he going to miss if he sat in an expensive restaurant?

As he sat up, the streetcar slowed to a stop in front of the Superdome. Roadside lights shined blue-and-yellow across the recessed entrances to the complex; some of the glow bathed the trunks of sidewalk palm trees. The nuns scurried down the aisle and out the back exit. The streetcar sat through two changes of the traffic signal while workers removed metal parade barricades from the side of the road. Joe bothered himself to read the billboards along the road. A Jägermeister ad showed a grimacing vampire who'd just sucked down a shot. To sell memberships at a new gym in the Central Business District, there was an enormous photo of a woman's perfect belly, suntanned and cut up so it looked like a chocolate bar; the bottom of her sports bra was dark with sweat.

The streetcar lurched into the intersection; as it turned, a new vista appeared through the front window: fewer buildings, fewer headlights, an open straightaway of road that seemed to disappear into the ashen sky. Just in front of the landscape's vanishing point, and far enough in the distance that Joe, without his glasses, couldn't make out the words on it, was a billboard. He identified its subject merely by recognizing its orange-and-black jumble of shapes. It was the first advertisement of the year for Scream in the Dark, the haunted house in Algiers, which would open at the end of the month. Any day now, Joe thought he could expect the fliers to come in the mail; they were postcards showing on their face the same orange-and-black shapes, and on the back a map of the route to take once you had crossed the Mississippi.

As Joe half-closed his eyes, so the screen of his eyeball was filled with skewed, flickering light, he pictured himself walking in the blue night past the orange-clad kids who worked there, strobing their flashlights across the gravel parking lot and the grassy path to the entrance.

Once you had paid and signed your release form, you were assigned a group number; you waited with your group in a long, low-roofed building full of metal chairs, listening to a recording of wails and creaking doors and lurid whispers that emanated from speakers mounted in corners of the building. During part of your wait, you had to watch a film about the mission of the church that sponsored Scream in the Dark.

Last year, Joe and Al had come to the haunted house after sneaking a few beers; Al's brother had given them the ride in his new Saturn, and he'd also given them the six-pack of Dixie. Instead of the traditional tunnel, which had served as the dark entrance for many years, last year you entered Scream in the Dark on your feet; you walked through a blazing red hallway, made a sharp left into a dark room from whose ceiling hung plastic-bagged cadavers. At regular intervals, a blue light began to illuminate the darkness, and all of the dead bodies started to sway, bouncing against you with a horrible plastic crackle. From the morgue, you entered upon a garage of rusted, abandoned cars; men covered from head to toe with black grease took slow steps toward you. There was yet another sharp turn once you exited the garage, a very abrupt right, and now, letting his eyes drift open as the rattling streetcar picked up speed, Joe remembered how Al, amid all the screams and clanks of metal, had grabbed hold of his hand and yanked him around the corner into the next dark corridor.

■

At Canal Street, the last stop, Joe stepped out the back door onto the sidewalk. There were people everywhere: blacks, many fewer whites, more women than men. The road had a sparkly, crushed-glass sheen. Fast-food signs were glittering, and stereo-camera-jewelry shops were blasting mellow love songs onto the trashy sidewalks: "Completely, wanna share my love," howled Michael Bolton.

Joe swung through the overlaps of people: hats, faces, chests, and arms peeling away as he made his way to his destination. A quartet of black girls, sweet and round-shouldered little fifth-grade girls, squeezed past him. "Hold the streetcar!" two of them shouted in unison. Their tiny voices trickled into the air.

"Streetcar!" Joe bellowed at his top voice, watching the girls dwindle into the crowd, their sugary voices swallowed up in the clamor. "Hold the streetcar!"

Another voice took up his cry: "Hold it, streetcar!" Then two more, and suddenly there were four guys in baggies and tank tops standing on the tracks, blocking the streetcar's route.

Joe watched until the first little girl climbed aboard.

Traffic crept by. In the opposite direction from the river, there was a cop barricade; above it, the black smoke of a fire hung. A bony rhythm track blew from the open windows of a passing white limo: it was Queen Latifah, rapping, "Just another day / living in the hood . . ."

He crossed Canal and didn't slow until he reached the second block of Bourbon, where a curbside brass band was playing. So the street was full of tourists, he thought. Big deal. It was still an amazing, forgiving street. It stretched in front of him like a hallway: cottages and storefronts and hotels leaning inward; the sky low and white, a ceiling. In dark windows and half alleys there were the pale faces of dealers and scammers. You could smell people on the air.

He was soaked up by the clapping crowd. They were dancing, close packed, shoulder to shoulder and arm in arm, necks wiggling and knees all liquidy, not like an audience at all. A bald black man was singing, "Sky is high / so am I . . ." Joe bent at his waist, hands on his knees, and listened to the music. After just a few moments, he felt the tune work its warm buzz up inside his spine. He smiled. He began pumping his foot up and down. He shook his ass as he stood to his full height and danced.

8:45 p.m.

As the van chugged slowly past a huddle of TV camera crews, Seth noted to himself with approval that his fellow jurors had improved their postures under the flat white glare of the reporters' lights. There was a stunned silence; Seth attributed it mostly to nerves, but he also thought that many of the jurors were going over the facts of the case in their heads so they'd be ready to face the media after the verdict was announced.

The van crept now into the half-circle driveway and up against the security entrance. The engine purred, and then stopped. Seth felt a calm kind of goodwill toward everyone in the van. There had been an outpouring of praise for his change of vote, and ultimately, after he'd explained his reasons, the tally had gone to twelve to zero against Rae Schipke. Being on the side of truth, or betterness, or however he wanted to put it, had made him bold and smart and vigorous.

The way he felt now was not something he'd forget real soon. He hoped.

They were all starting to whisper now, and the sliding panel door opened, letting in a rush of fresh air, and then suddenly, in one simultaneous, disorienting moment, a dozen or more cameras rushed the van, and Rita, who sat beside him on the back bench, put her lips wetly against his ears and whispered.

Seth giggled. "That *tickles*," he said.

"I want you to call me," she said in a voice that was distinct but still low enough that only he could hear it. "I wanna get together with you baby, when this is over."

His spine shivered, and his prong began to stiffen. He said, "I will. I'll call you. Absolutely."

9 : 2 5   p . m .

Joe's footsteps went *wunk wunk* as he turned off Royal onto a quieter street that was crazy-full of water—water dripping off roofs, off balconies, puddling in the center of the street as if, just before his approach, the block had been singled out by half a typhoon. Lamplight spilled apple green across the sidewalk; the color mutated into oily rainbows where it bled down the curb and into the rushing gutters. Level with Joe's shoulders, loose wires that were interwoven with sugary-smelling vines drooped along the facades of one building after the next, like spiderwebs spouting from the mortar between crumbling bricks. The trail of wire and weed disappeared finally into the dark portal of a store that sold antique bottles; blue ones and green ones and sparkly red ones that sat on shelves in the front windows, glowing with the weak light of a few fluorescent bulbs deep within the store. The store's entryway was shrouded in steam.

Weirded out by the uninhabitedness, Joe came to a stop, scratching his sole across the gritty sidewalk in imitation of a soldier's lockstep. This was prime pavement for some kind of ambush, he thought; gunplay; no witnesses around, just laughter floating across the rooftops from Bourbon Street in one direction and steam whistles and tug horns from the Mississippi River in the other. Every single day, without exception, a couple of people got their faces shot off around town. Graffiti writers kept a log of the victims' names on the support pillars of the highway overpasses. Actual murder was rare in the Quarter, but still you had to keep your watch.

He hooked his arm around a droplet-covered street lamp and leaned into the street. At the far end of the block there was an old oak tree with a huge trunk, just behind the fence of a shuttered hotel. Its quivering branches dipped to the sidewalk. The leaves skittered with soothing rhythm across the cement. As Joe watched, mesmerized by the folding and unfolding of the tree, a figure in dark clothing emerged from within the branches and leaves. It moved lightly and quickly and implacably toward him as if it were an animated figure projected from a hidden machine onto the street. It carried an umbrella with a high, elegant arch. Its footsteps rang like horseshoes. It seemed to drag the fog and oak leaves with it as it walked. Its head was up and its shoulders were squared formally and it took sharp, loud intakes of breath.

Man or woman? Joe wondered. The face wasn't covered or veiled; just dark. He couldn't make out the curves of its torso, if there were any.

"Hey," he said in what he hoped was an offhand, unworried voice as he loosened his grip on the lamppost and began walking toward the stranger. He was within a dozen steps of it when it turned suddenly and slipped into the alley that was in the middle of the block, just across the street from Nola, the restaurant where he was meeting White Donna.

The street roared with silence as Joe stood in place for a moment, looking at the pillows of fog that tumbled along the gutters. Tucking his forearms against his ribs, he threw himself into a run. The hardness of the street surged gratifyingly through the muscles and bones of his legs. As he rounded into the mouth of the cobblestone alley where the figure had gone, his heart skipped a beat and the pit of his stomach reddened. He slowed to a walk, pressing his hand to the center of his chest. Making his way to the dead end of the alley, he surveyed the landscape, looking up and down the walls of shuttered doors and windows; his eye lingered at each of the shadowy, hooded doorways. After a moment, he moved toward a dark vestibule at the top of a half flight of stairs. Dim light glowed from within the building; it spilled through busted wooden shutter slats onto the cement landing at the top of the steps.

He thought at first that the familiar tapping noise that he heard as he climbed was the sound of his own footsteps, but when he came to a stop on the landing the *click clang* continued, and he twisted his head to see the dark figure, its umbrella resting tight to its head and its legs hidden by the steam that burbled from the grated water-runoff duct, running up the alley away from him. In the time it took Joe to lunge down the stairs, the figure had made its escape around the corner.

He paid a moment of empty attention to the cobblestones at his feet, blank headed as if the shrouded figure had run off with his thoughts. After a few minutes had passed, he stomped up the alley, thumping his flat palm on the puffy seats of a dozen motorcycles that were chained along the wall.

As he came out of the alley, hunching his face down and lifting his T-shirt to wipe the sweat from his forehead and nose, he noticed that the street was different than it had been a few minutes earlier. There were couples and groups humming along the sidewalks, and a tall man in black tie was blowing discordant notes out of his tiny saxophone. Stepping into the street, Joe let his shirt fall back over his belly, and then he took an abrupt hop backwards to avoid a delivery girl—flash of legs and elbows and insulated red pizza carrier—who whistled almost silently past him on her bike.

"Iquoi!" he called after her with admiration in his voice. "Girl, what's up!"

The bike stopped on a dime. The girl's tentative voice floated back to him: "Joe Keith?"

"Yeah!" He sprinted over to her, splashing through a milky green puddle in the center of the street. He leaned up against her bike, a black Schwinn Cruiser with whitewalls and, beneath the torn banana seat, hefty shock absorbers. "Baby," he said, "I haven't seen you since like forever."

"How hard've you been sweatin' me?" she said, breaking into her usual exuberant smile. "I've totally been around."

Iquoi was part Indian and part Irish, with shoulder-length black hair; tonight she wore it in beaded pigtails. Her thick lips always gleamed with purple or black lipstick, and she had creamy cheeks and a long, muscley neck. She wore a black sports bra under baggy green cutoff overalls, and blue suede Pumas with no socks.

"Just 'cause you've been around doesn't mean that I have."

"Hard-ass. You wanna tell me where you been keepin' your tired self?"

"At school! It started again."

"How'm I to know? Pretty bitches there?"

"They work some serious runway on the greens of Country Day, I dare say. Bitches in platform sandals and beaded tops."

"Mall clothes? *Melrose Place* clothes?"

"No indeed. These are *rich* girls. I go to school with rich girls who buy their clothes at pissy little stores in Houston over their summer vacation."

"You dating any of them?" She leaned into him so the thick denim bib of her overalls chafed against his thin T-shirt.

"Not that I know of."

"Have you ever made out with any of those girls?"

" 'Course."

"Do they kiss as good as me?" she asked, leaning just a fifteenth of an inch closer and opening her mouth on Joe's.

As the tip of her tongue tickled along the inside of his cheek, Joe shut his eyes and saw a vista of glittering silver stars against the blue inside of his lids. He got a hard-on that jutted sideways; the head of his dick, thinly cloaked by his baggy, handkerchief-weight shorts, lodged on the sloping handlebar that was jammed sideways between his and Iquoi's waists. He slid his hand up his thigh and cupped the wayward dick in his palm.

"I'm disarmed," Iquoi whispered, and kissed his neck, and cupped her palm over the back of his hand; her thumb nudged the inside of his thigh.

From somewhere on an adjacent block, a girl's sweet voice sang five pure notes, *"I wish you heaven,"* and then dissolved into the night.

"How's that?" He kissed her neck and lifted their hands away from his subsiding erection. He put his other hand, flat, inside the front of her coveralls, on her bare stomach. As her breath came, he stepped his fingers along her ribs.

"It smells like it rained," she said as his hand came to rest on the underside of her breast. "How come I'm not wet? God, it smells so sweet."

"It smells nice," he said, "but I think it's maybe like *you*. You smell nice." Out of the corner of his eye, Joe saw a solitary red cloud tumble across the black sky. "I feel like this is my like lucky night."

"Could be. You look good tonight. You don't have a very wholesome look. I think you've lost all your baby fat."

"Shit, yeah." He hitched up the side of his T-shirt to show off his ribs, which were plainly visible.

"Keep your clothes on, baby. I gotta haul. I got food to deliver; that's the essence of my nighttime."

"I wish we could hang out sometime soon."

"Make an effort, Joe. That's all you gotta do." She adjusted her hands on the rubber grips at the ends of the handlebars.

"I totally will. I'm making changes in my life. I'm breaking into some new shit with the way I handle myself."

"I can tell."

Joe took his hand away from the nape of her neck. "Give me a thrill, Iquoi. Spin me a pop fly."

"Climb aboard."

"Cool." Joe hopped up onto the handlebars, propping his feet on the front wheel guard. He crossed his arms over his chest, leaned back so the top of his head rested on Iquoi's arm, and looked up at the blurry sky.

"You settled?" she asked.

"Hit it."

She sighed, and stood up to get more pedaling momentum. The bike quickly accelerated, whizzing through the murky green night. Just before they reached the intersection with Decatur, Iquoi whistled a sweet, round *O* sound, and the front tire lifted off the ground.

When Joe ducked inside the restaurant after a final kiss from Iquoi, he was swallowed up in an abundance of blond, broad-shouldered guys in suits who towered over their girlfriends. All of them were gleamingly suntanned and toothy, with immaculate brows. They exuded a foamy, expensive, green spice and spoke with chummy disrespect for one another. Joe squeezed past the shoulders until he was at the front of the crowd, face to face with the mod reservation table and the elevators that lifted you to the dining rooms on the second and third floors.

He raised his hand in greeting to the strapping, sunburned host behind the lectern. "Hey, Leon."

"What's up," the guy said, beckoning Joe with a finger as, with his other hand, he casually scribbled into the open reservation book. A couple of years back, Leon had worked in a restaurant that Joe's dad managed. It had been a piss-elegant, black-tie kind of dining room; Leon was a little too casual to pass under Daddy's eye, so he hadn't worked there for long.

"Nothing's up," Joe said, dropping his elbows on the lectern and leaning. "I'm meeting some people for dinner." He flipped the toe of his sneaker against the floor, bouncing in time to the Janet Jackson candy that was playing over the sound system. "Can you comp me a beer?"

"Do these people you're with have a reservation? Who are they? I hope they're grown-ups."

"Yeah, they're adults or whatever."

Leon looked him right in the eye. "Your whole face is smeared with lipstick. Looks like war paint, dude." He bunched a napkin in his hand, dipped it in a glass of ice water, and passed it to Joe. "Here."

"I appreciate it," Joe said, and stepped to the side of Leon's station to wipe his face. He glanced around the room, trying to find White Donna. He made eye contact with as many cuties as he could until his gaze came to rest on the corner table in the back where she sat with her boyfriend, Black Chris.

The sight of familiar faces gladdened him, and he lifted his hand over his head and waved to them. Silvery bubbles of keyboard and rhythm guitar propelled him past the clinking tabletops and beneath the fussing arms of waitresses and waiters and water servers. He had a special hang to his walk: shoulders slouched back, arms loose.

Donna applauded his arrival. Joviality radiated from the tips of her fingers. "Hey, hey," she said as he plopped down in the seat across from her. She wiggled her shoulders and sang along with the song in her mind: "There were plant and birds and rocks and things . . ."

"Hey." Joe cracked his knuckles. "Almost didn't make y'all out without my glasses."

"Hey sweets," Donna said. "I didn't know you wore glasses."

"Secret. I'm starved."

"So are we."

"Lookin' good, Joe," smirked Donna's boyfriend, Black Chris, who was a rich med school student from Mobile. "Your face looks kind of red. Kind of made up."

Joe hiccuped a laugh and then said, "I had a little fun before I got here. Does it look like sunburn, or what does it look like?"

"It doesn't in any way resemble sunburn," Chris said. "Not like the sunburn that results from the sun that shines on this planet."

"Moody," Joe grumbled through a smile.

"It's festive in here," Donna said, turning her bottle of beer upside down to demonstrate that it was empty. "We don't care if Joe's a little bit made up, do we?"

"We care somewhat," Chris said.

"Don't be so *dry*, bitch," Donna said. She made a small nod in the direction of her empty Abita bottle.

"Let me drink in the fierce sight of you," Joe said. Donna had a sleek new look for dinner. She was dressed in an Adidas-striped black slip that was styled after a b-ball tank top. Her shoulders were tough, rounded, and you could discern the fine line of her upper body, especially just below her arms, where her back fanned with muscle—enough to notice, not too much. She had removed this afternoon's hair extensions and slicked back her true, short locks with a pomade that smelled like metal.

"She looks fine," Chris said, "doesn't she? I don't know how I got so lucky—not being from here or anything."

"You look totally beautiful," Joe told Donna.

"Thank you, sweetie. I totally try. Sometimes, when I'm bored, I'll spend an extra amount of time getting my look together or whatever. I wasn't bored today, though. Actually, strike all that shit I just said; I'm hardly ever bored."

"How come? I am."

"Because I'm an imposter in a teenage industry. I'm in rock and roll radio. I want to work in movies. Everything I want to do with my life is like tied into teenagers in an aggravating way. See, *you're* allowed to get bored with whatever band you wanna get bored with, even if they're completely the hippest band that ever existed. You're allowed to say that you don't give a shit about Doom or Myst. But I'm not. If I did, it would be this indication that I'm not *immersed* in the culture of teen. I have to be this entirely enthusiastic faux teen. I mean, I can't troll around in a linen suit or any shit like that; you know, silk stockings and pearls and a cream-colored hat. I don't think so."

"She's having misgivings," said Chris. "But I respect you, baby. Fuck if I'm not fifty grand into medical school and I don't exactly feel aglow with purpose and industry and all that. Like I'm in a lab, and I look at my hands, and I get lost in this reverie, and when I come out of it I realize that I'm just a little speck. I mean, I'm going to help people. I really am going to be like a good person. But I'm not going to be large."

Joe made a few sympathetic sounds in the back of his mouth. A few months ago, he'd had a crush on Chris that he'd tried without success to hide. He'd never been around a guy who was so casually successful in school and yet looked so fine. A guy like that existed in sublime relief against the sky, Joe thought. This evening, Chris was practically shirtless beneath his casual plaid jacket; he wore his shirt unbuttoned and drawn off his cut chest. His sunburned neck was choked by a strap of leather from which hung a silver ring, a brass skeleton key, and the shellacked jaw of a small fish. On his chin, three dozen spines of short beard grew in concentric circles. His short dreads were always fastidiously knotted and redolent of vanilla oil.

"We're not always so dissatisfied," Donna said, leaning away from the table as a waiter exchanged her beer bottle. "For me, I'm actually happy to be making some dough in a job that's not in a killer office with fluorescent lights, and I come home to a sweet boyfriend, when he's not at the hospital or at school, and he gives me some love in our big apartment with furniture we like."

"We have nice furniture," Chris agreed, crossing his arms over his chest. He kept his bemused, infuriating gaze on Joe.

"Hey, hey, Joe. Tell me you've looked over those books I gave you."

Joe looked at the table. "Not *yet*."

"Speak up, son."

"Bullshit."

"Speak with reverence."

"Oh my God."

"Did you look through the college catalogs?"

"Not yet."

"The SAT guide?"

"Not yet?"

"The ACT guide?"

"Not hardly."

"Slacker."

"Duh."

"I'm not laughing, son."

"Well, what've you been doing with yourself? Let's get off the subject of me."

"What else do I do? A lot of school. Loads. Too many labs, for one thing. Hard-ass lab partners for another. Micromanage everything so we each do the exact same amount of work. They don't take rest—"

"As if you'd take a rest," Donna said gently. She passed the fresh Abita from one hand to the other before taking a draw on it.

"And I'm applying for residencies, working out—which, by the way, is something we need to talk about. I haven't seen your ass at the gym . . ."

Joe covered his face with his hand. "Tomorrow afternoon. I'm going tomorrow, man. You gonna be there tomorrow?"

"Yeah I'm gonna be there tomorrow. You ain't gonna have a body on you if you don't make it like regular clockwork priority. At least four days a week, Joe. Two hours a session. An hour of cardio work—"

"Okay, okay."

"You relent really easily," Donna said. "He hasn't succeeded in draggin' my butt down there. I don't want all of those endorphins pulsing through me. They'd freak out my natural languor. Ya hear me?"

"My girl here," Chris said, flicking a thumb at Donna, "she keeps me out at night. Old peoples like us, I think we need our sleep."

"Have you done any celebrating of your birthday?" Donna asked, rearranging her silverware into geometric shapes, pinging fork tines against spoon beds.

A waitress appeared at the side of the table. She placed a bottle of Rolling Rock in front of Joe. "Compliments of Leon," she said.

Joe looked up at her. "Cool. Thanks. Ask him to come talk to us if he gets a chance." A grin swelled up from his chest. There was nothing like being treated with some respect. He realized that his progress was glacial, but still he was making the first moves into being a citizen of the world. He leaned across the table. "I had a very mellow birthday, which is the usual kind of birthday I have. It always coincides with this guy at school's birthday, a very cool guy named Arling, and him and me got together with some guys and played putt-putt. It's some tradition we've had for a couple of years. It's totally a good time." He swigged on the beer and then he asked, "What're you guys going to eat?"

Donna pointed at the open menu before her. "You wanna split some stuff? I wanna load up."

"Yeah." Joe nodded. "Yeah." He thrummed his fingertips across the tablecloth in time to the gassy Dr. John that was shaking from the speakers.

"I'm just having a salad," Chris said. His neck flexed as if it were a single muscle.

"You don't look fat any more," Joe said. "How come you're still on a diet?"

Chris pulled his jacket farther open. "How do you think I look the way I look? I wasn't *fat*. I was bulking up."

"Oy," Donna said. "Some people are like caught up in paroxysms of self-regard."

"Yeah," Joe said.

"How much should we spend, sweetie?"

"Well, you were giving Kel shit this afternoon about her budgetizing."

"You were what?" Chris asked.

Donna pouted dismissively. "We're not having this category of conversation. I'm too hungry to discuss budgets and who should be on them. I'm not my mother yet, unfortunately or whatever."

"You're getting close, though," Chris said sweetly, his eyes overflowing with admiration.

Joe's face warmed up as he watched Chris take his girlfriend's hand and bring it to his lips. His brainwaves bounced against his skull in a kind of dazzling mix of generosity and lonesomeness. *Kiss her*, he said to himself. *Kiss her. Kiss me.* Somebody.

In just the nick of time, the waitress sidled up to the table with a laugh on her face and offered to explain the night's special dishes.

■

For Joe and Donna, dinner was tossed salad in a kicky, fatty, anchovy-and-jalapeño dressing, roasted garlic and plum tomato pizza, salmon strips with a ginger dipping sauce, sour creamy mashed potatoes. Joe drank two more Rolling Rocks.

Donna had four more Abitas. Chris sipped iced tea. For dessert, there was a three-way split of banana cream pie à la moded with chocolate ice cream.

Joe washed away the sweet taste with a mouthful of Chris's iced tea and then sauntered to the bar and bought a pack of Camel Wides, the brand that all of his Country Day newbies smoked when they weren't in training for their sport. The bar was an *L* on the far side of the elevator bank. There were no stools in front of it, but it was crowded anyway. Joe had to turn sideways and squeeze between patrons to grab a pack of matches.

"I couldn't stay in my seat," a man said loudly in his ear. Joe turned and saw that it was one of the husky, coiffed guys who'd been waiting in the entryway when he first arrived at the restaurant. Now the husky guy's tie was loosened and his shirt billowed out of his pants waist. He was propped against the bar like a canoe. "I ate too much. I mean, I ate so much that I'm gonna have stretch marks. What'd you have for dessert, man?"

"Banana cream pie."

"Why goddamnit I'd like to have a piece of banana cream pie. Why didn't I think of that?"

Joe lit a match and dropped it in an ashtray the size of a hubcap.

"I had crème caramel," the man said. "My God, that mother was tasty. But I'm gonna be fat! It oozed past my lips without even hesitating at all, a frickin' bucket of the goo. Sheesh. Down my throat and into my belly."

"Whoa."

"Look at this belly." The man pointed at himself.

"Not so bad," Joe said.

"You're a good kid."

"Nah."

"Yeah, you are. I can see that plain as day."

Joe punched a cigarette out of the pack and held it between his thumb and forefinger. He fixed his eye on the man's jacket lapel. "Let me ask you something."

"Hurry up and ask me before I blow up right here in this bar. Damn, I feel fat."

"What are you guys all wearing? All of you guys smell really fresh?"

The man stuck his fist in his pants pocket and jingled his change and keys. "You wanna know what it is that makes us smell the way we do. Do I understand you correctly?"

"Yeah. That's the question I'm asking you."

"You're asking this glutton?"

"Yeah." Losing interest for a moment, Joe glanced at the silent TV that hung from the ceiling behind the bar. It showed footage of flames blowing high into the air as they engulfed a three-story building. The screen changed then to show a casually attired reporter who stood in front of smoking rubble; just below his stomach, the word LIVE flashed in red. Joe turned back to the glutton, who wore a patient face.

"Lime," the man said.

"Lime?"

"I smell like lime juice. Us guys use it on our hair to keep it looking like this, to keep it blond, to keep it moist, to keep it smelling so fine." He used the index finger and thumb of each hand to comb the precise part on the side of his full head of hair. "I'm gonna take my leave," he said. "Think I'm gonna order a piece of that banana cream pie."

"Take a bite for me, man."

"Fair enough," the man said gravely, drifting away from the bar.

Joe got his cigarette started and returned his attention to the TV, which now showed a reporter standing outside a brightly lighted satellite van. At the bottom of the screen, in small black print, were the words SHAW VERDICT. The footage changed to show three small boys in identical suits being led across a crowded street, then changed back to the reporter. After the reporter talked for a while, the screen flashed and changed to show highlights of the trial that Joe had been seeing for weeks.

His loneliness was like a radioactive disk in his stomach, sending its trace elements all over his body. In the midst of fun and noise and lights, you could still feel like no one was waiting for you, no one had your name kind of reverberating in his head. He kept his gaze on the TV for another couple of minutes, and then he looked at his stupid, bony hands.

"You need another beer?"

"Um, no, but can I use the phone?" Joe asked the bartender.

"There's a pay phone back at the bathrooms."

"Please, dude. I'm too comfortable to move."

The bartender sighed. "Come around the side; I'll pass it to you."

Joe stubbed out his cigarette and made his way to an empty yard of bar, where the bartender set him up with a portable phone. He fingered through his wallet until he found the business card that Seth had given him on the evening they'd fucked around at the New Orleans Athletic Center.

Keep an eye on the trial, Joe remembered him saying; *call me when it's over.* Maybe Seth meant it, maybe he didn't, but only a weak little pussy coward would be afraid to make the thirty-second phone call.

He dialed both of the numbers on the card and left short messages that included the number of his personal line at home; then he called his mom.

"Hey," he said when she answered, "I'm late."

"I've got the clock right in front of me."

"Are you pissed?"

"I am."

"Don't be mad at me, Mom."

"Just get home now. Where are you?"

"I'm eating. These people I know are gonna give me a ride home."

"What people?"

"The girl is a DJ and the guy's in med school at Tulane."

"Joe . . ."

"Mom, you can go to sleep. I promise I'm on my way really soon. I love you, Mom."

"Of course it's same here."

He hung up and slid the phone to the waiting bartender and thanked him. On his way back to Donna and Chris, he bumped into the waitress.

"What's up?" she said.

"Hey," he said. They walked arm in arm the rest of the way to his table. "Are we gonna stay for another beer?" he asked Donna as he sat down.

"We totally can, I guess," Donna said.

"We're totally staying for another beer," he told the waitress.

"I'm totally psyched," the waitress said. "One Rolling Rock and one Abita?"

"Truly," Donna said.

Chris narrowed his eyes and sank back in his chair. "Who was that guy at the bar?"

"A cool guy."

"You know him?"

"I do now."

"Did you hit on him or did he hit on you?"

"Neither."

"You know, you can't let grown-up guys make a move on you."

"Why not?"

"You're six-fucking-teen."

Donna reached across the table to grab Joe's pack of Wides. She bumped one from the pack and held it to her nose and broke into a coughing fit. "Joe," she said, "the only concern we have is that you don't do anything reckless. I know, even as I sit here and say it, that my like admonition is ludicrous, given my own fucked lifestyle. But me and Chris have consciences, you know. And we need to assuage them. You just be as careful as you absolutely can."

"Yeah," Chris said.

"You guys have good hearts," Joe said to the tablecloth. "I mean it. But I think it's dumb for you to lecture me." When he looked up, the two of them were sharing a hungry French kiss.

"Solly," Donna said after a moment, putting her thumb on Chris's lips to turn his head away.

"You wanna go dancing?" Joe asked, pressing his palms against his knees. The symphonic hustle gusting out of the sound system had put a wiggle in his spine.

"We're very foxy dancers," Donna said. "That's what we've been told."

"By my *mother*." Chris laughed. "I don't know that she's exactly like a dance critic."

"Who cares? She has an eye. I mean, she can tell we're good together."

"Yeah," Joe said, popping from his seat. "I wanna boogie with you. C'mon. Let's go dancing and shit. I'm already totally late for my curfew."

"We're gonna give you a ride home," Chris said. "We'll get you there safe."

"So let's dance. If you guys aren't too cool to swing by Oz with me. That guy Welk is gonna be there."

"Oh?" Donna said.

"Shut up."

"That guy Welk," Donna said, leaning into the aisle to catch the attention of the passing waitress, "isn't at Oz, baby."

"Really," Joe said, his stomach plummeting as if it had been knotted to a fifty-pound weight and tossed out a window.

"Really," Donna said. "That guy Welk is so much closer than you think. Look over your shoulder, sweetie. Across the room, luv. Right inside the door."

Joe obeyed. The hairs along his brow tingled. Grains of itchy sweat pushed through the pores on his nose and chin. His view of the entrance was obscured by all of the sea-foamy broad-shouldered guys, who were now pushing their way out of the restaurant, gathering their girls and arranging a variety of ball caps on their heads, but when Joe finally did see Welk—in jeans and a green Tulane T-shirt—standing casually just inside the door, his eyesight corrected itself to twenty-twenty and he swayed on his feet. He had a big grin on his face. He knew it. He didn't care that it was oafish. Fuck if he cared that it wasn't very sophisticated at all.

The room was dusky, lighted only by the small halogen lamp that sat on Mrs. Shaw's mahogany desk. On the silent TV screen against the far wall, two young boys threw green glop at each other. The gunk hung from their shoulders; it coated their chests and heads. Whichever boy was greenest at the end of the allotted time lost. It was one of Rae Schipke's favorite shows, and now she watched it from her perch on the leather couch in the library of the Shaw Foundation headquarters. She was, at the same time, listening on the phone to Darcy Favrot, her personal lawyer.

He was telling her that the jury was on its way back to court, that contradictory rumors were circulating about the verdict. "We need you and Mrs. Shaw within the half hour," he said.

"One fucking half hour?"

"I'm not the judge," Favrot squeaked indignantly. "I'm simply telling you the situation."

"You are on my list," Rae warned. "And it wouldn't surprise me at all if there was a hung jury."

"I'm sorry," he said pointedly, "I couldn't understand what you just said."

"So cautious."

"Prudent."

"You know I keep the security on my phone."

"And I know you tape all of your calls. Rae, I know you."

"Enough of this. Forget it."

"Once you are exonerated, I will."

"That's sweet, but you're still on my list."

"I don't want to have this conversation. Rae, get a hold on yourself. And put on something sweet, please. Can't you wear a ribbon in your hair?"

With her laughter, she sprayed saliva on the phone mouthpiece and her hand. "A ribbon? And knickers, too?"

"Rae . . ."

"Darcy, you're *such* an asshole. I mean, a *ribbon?*"

"For the TV?"

"I know *why,* but *me?* Do you think I own one item of sweet clothing? I've got that Chloe petticoat, darling, but that's for my wedding day if it ever comes. Nah. Oh, shit, I'll just, you know, wear what I'm wearing. It's awfully late in the game for a rehabilitation of my image."

Favrot chuckled.

"Darcy?"

On TV, the competing boys burst balloonfuls of red liquid against a brick wall. The sight nearly took Rae's breath away.

"Darcy?" she said again.

"I'm sorry," he sputtered, "I got water up my nose."

"Are you in the pool?"

"I'm getting *out*. I'll surely beat you to court."

"I paid for that pool."

"So you seem to think."

"I *paid* for that pool."

"How is the Myrtha?"

"Her?"

"Yes. Is she lucid this eve?"

"What do you think? She tried to do a somersault on the gravel driveway. *I* had to carry her."

Darcy snickered. "Pale, elegant," he murmured. "The Myrtha knew how to dress for court back in the days. Hats and gloves. A parasol."

"Suck it up, baby. I'll see you in forty-five minutes."

"*Twenty*-five."

"You'll wait." Rae disconnected the call and tossed the phone against the exposed-brick wall with as much strength as she could muster in her sitting position. It clattered to the hard tile floor, unbroken. "Plastic," she marveled to herself. "So perfect."

A long slate hallway led from the library, where Rae sat, to the master bedroom wing, where Mrs. Shaw waited. A moment after the phone hit the wall, Mrs. Shaw's voice rumbled from the bowels of the house, a mess of indecipherable sounds.

"You're on my list, too," Rae muttered, patting her belly, which was encased in a red leather dress. She was ready for the verdict. Her bare legs had just been waxed; they were sun-tanned and strong. The pain in her ankle had subsided with the help of steroid injections.

If Seth had succeeded, she'd have her freedom for a while longer—long enough to disappear while there were no judgments against her name or local investments. Her house was in order now, as it hadn't been when the charges were first filed. Tomorrow, she'd be on her way to Brazil. She looked forward to spending the rest of her life in that heat, with the pick of all those street urchins selling themselves for pennies.

Mercy me, she said to herself, and slapped her palms on her lap before groaning to her feet.

She went across the room to the intercom on the wall and patched through to Mrs. Shaw's room. "Get yourself dressed, Myrtha! I'm calling the car around. You've got"—she looked at her watch—"fourteen minutes." Before Mrs. Shaw could answer, Rae strutted into the chill of the dark hall. The slate was like ice beneath her bare feet. She broke into a run toward her office, past louvered doors that opened onto other hallways. Where all the halls met there was a black marble swimming pool that hadn't been cleaned in months.

Rae karate-kicked open her office door. "You're on my list, honey!" she shouted to the empty room, making a visual sweep of dark furniture draped with clothing. She passed around the corner of her desk and dropped into the chair. "Can I get some help in here?" she whispered to herself.

Sounding like a flock of seagulls, Mrs. Shaw's voice carried into the room.

Rae looked through her purse with single-mindedness. *What have we here?* Eight thousand dollars in twenties, rubber-banded; her electric Rolodex; Cinn-A-Burst gum; rubbers; a cap gun; a real handgun; loose bullets and paper clips; the business card of the plastic surgeon in Houston whom she planned to visit in the a.m. for a command performance.

She held the card close to her face. *Dr. Shaun Martines.*

The prissiness of the type on his card turned her stomach. He was the man to whom she'd lost her virginity; if only he'd become something huge, someone important. Still, given the circumstances of their first meeting, it thrilled Rae to remember all of the times in ensuing years that they'd gotten together for intimate dinners and dancing.

Shaun, Shaun . . .

She'd been a late bloomer, twenty when she boned him. She was his student teacher at the now-defunct Corcoran Country Day School in a suburb of Houston. He was in ninth grade. After sex in her dorm room, they went out for breakfast. In the little family restaurant, they appraised one another across the Formica tabletop. God, Rae thought, he's so much more elegant than me; God his fingernails are immaculate and his brush cut is so well kept and he wears the most sumptuously tight blue jeans and he carries his keys on a silver chain that he bought in Panama.

But breakfast hadn't ended well. She could tell that he didn't love her, didn't respect her. He pushed aside his tray of oatmeal and sliced fruit, rested his chin on the table, and studied her as she ate. Slowly, his face became a mask of distaste; he looked at her as if she were an animal in a cage, rending tendon from bone.

"How come you eat with your mouth open?" he asked. "How come you don't have a man who's your own age? How come you wanna be a teacher?"

Rae put her yolk-stained slice of toast beside her fried egg, gripped the plate in her left hand, and broke it against the top of his head. The pieces showered across the tabletop and floor, and he spat a sliver of tongue that had been bitten off at the moment of the plate's impact.

"Ah cah beweave oo id at," he said.

■

Now she pulled the phone from its base on the desk and dialed. When Seth's machine answered, she entered his four-digit security code and listened to the messages.

Hey, this is Jed. I have the check for you. I need to know how you want it made out before I put it in the mail. Call me at Royal Games. Ask for the red phone. If they won't put you through, then try to get through on the green phone. *Don't* let them put you on the blue phone. Okay? Red phone or green phone, but not blue.

Rae erased the message and listened for the next.

I'm waiting to hear from you, Seth. Now that we've dropped the charges, I think it's time for a little healing. We love you, honey. We want you to call us. Please, please call us at your convenience. You can get me after seven.

Parents, Rae guessed. Delete. Next message.

Seth, this is Joe. This is Joe Keith. I'm a little bit drunk or whatever, and I'm thinking about you. You were so much fun. You were, totally. I want to go swimming again with you! Every time I walk through the NOAC I think about the wicked times we had—or I mean time. Whatever. I wanna see you again. Um, shit, you said to give you a call when that trial was over. So, I'm like giving you a call. I would really like to get together again. Would it be like a lie to say I miss you? Anytime you want. Really. If you like get a chance soon, give *me* a call at my house. Tonight, dude, would be very cool. Here's my number in case you lost it.

Oh, but *I* remember, Rae said to herself. She replayed the message. *I want to go swimming again with you! Every time I walk through the NOAC I think about the wicked times we had.* She remembered catching Seth and the boy in a clutch by the pool. Seth was wrapped in a towel, pretending he barely knew the boy. She replayed the message again. *If you like get a chance soon, give* me *a call at my house. Tonight, dude, would be very cool.*

Here's my number in case you lost it. As Rae jotted the number on a slip of paper, she made the decision to leave the message intact on Seth's machine.

She put the phone down and drew open the bottom desk drawer, which was deep enough to hold a couple of dozen file folders and a stack of thick books. She pulled out the current white pages as well as *Polk's City Directory.* She ran her fingers along the spine of each book, and then she checked the white pages. The boy's name and number were listed without an address, so she pushed the white pages onto the floor and opened the *Polk's.* It was divided into three sections, each of which was organized by a different variable: street name and number, last name, phone number. If you were rich, or public, you knew about *Polk's* and could ask to be left out; most people were neither. Rae turned to the phone listings and ran her thumb down the numbers until she found the boy's. She scribbled his address and looked at the *Polk's* entry again. There was a Sherry Keith at the same address, with a different phone number. Rae scribbled the second number and drew parentheses around it. She'd read that name before. She closed her eyes, to concentrate. *Sherry Keith.* After a few minutes, she opened her eyes. She was drawing a blank.

Insurance, she told herself, and tucked the slip of paper in her purse. Can I help it if I'm not a trusting woman? She rose from her seat and cocked her head to listen.

Tip, tee, tip . . .

Mrs. Shaw's voice whistled through the air. This time, her words were quite clear: "My weeping friends I left behind," she shrilled. The tapping of her cane grew nearer.

"Myrtha," Rae called across the room. "I'm sorry to rush you. I'm sorry to speak so crossly."

In the darkness just outside the office door, Mrs. Shaw's face appeared. "I'm ready darling," she said.

11:00 p.m.

It turned out that a man everybody knew, a man named Marcus McNair, was having a blowout in the empty storage space above his junk shop on Decatur Street. Donna, who'd been to previous parties in the same space, led the way down the dark alley that ran beside the building. At the very back of the alley, she shoved a door open and held it with her shoulder as Chris, Joe, and Welk entered into a small foyer that glowed with green light. The foyer was actually just the first-floor landing of a narrow flight of stairs. Music shook the walls of the stairway, and, when he put his hand on the slippery metal banister, the bones in Joe's fingers and wrist and jaw shivered.

Chris wasn't waiting for anybody; he took the stairs two at a time, darting through the slouching party traffic that clotted the entrance. Joe couldn't make himself follow; he stood on the first step, looking up at the broad backs of a half dozen men who were smoking cigars. The men wore matching gun holsters, the stitching of which glowed in the dark.

With a touch all its own, Welk's belt buckle pressed against the small of Joe's back. Then his stubbled chin and neck came to rest on the dip where Joe's neck met his shoulder, and the wet inside of his lips pressed against Joe's cheek, and his voice whispered into Joe's ear: "You sure you wanna go upstairs? You sure?"

"Don't you?" Joe asked.

"It'd be cool to just stand here in the dark, I think. Don't you?" Welk's voice was slow with beer and cigarettes.

"Right here?"

"Yeah right here." His tongue lapped the underside of Joe's chin. "You taste good."

"Hey, do I?"

"I'd love to hear you say my name in that sexy voice of yours, dude."

My voice? My stupid, stupid voice? "Hey, Welk."

"Hey, Joe."

"Hey, Welk."

"Hey."

"Hey."

"I like the way that sounds coming out of you. I can feel it rumbling up your back." Welk's hands joined; the knuckles of his thumbs dug tight into Joe's belly. His arms were like hard rubber coils around Joe, and the feeling of being enfolded in them made the veins in Joe's legs and the nerve endings along his spine burst into flame. In his dick there were a hundred million rapturous explosions going off. It was amazing to him that he could actually move his hands, his stupid, useless hands, so just for the fuck of it he rubbed his palms along Welk's forearms, smoothing the light hair in one direction and then the other, even as Welk's fingers were nimbly unzipping his shorts and undoing the top button and the flat of Welk's hand was pressing against his belly and Welk's fingertips were pinching the elastic of his boxers.

With a muted gasp, Welk pulled Joe's backside tight against him and lifted him up in the air. "Joe, man," he whispered. "Fuck, man, you're so fine. Man, you smell so good." As he returned Joe to his feet, a couple of his fingers hunted farther into the boxers.

Joe blew out a sharp laugh. "That tickles."

"*Tickles?*" His voice was incredulous, disappointed.

Suddenly, with a gust of warm, damp air, the door beside them burst open and just as quickly slammed shut, and more bodies joined the dark green loiterers in the stairwell.

One of the newcomers was Donna, who burbled, "Look who showed up. I found her traipsing down the alley like a little ho."

"Keep on talking, girl, and I'll keep on recording your defamation for my lawsuit," Kel said giddily. "Joe, Welk, hi; it's me."

"Hey," Joe said. "What's up, Kel?"

Welk loosened his grip on Joe and leaned across the darkness to kiss her—on the lips, from the sound of it.

"I have bag," Kel whispered. "You want a taste?" Welk let go of Joe—just like that, let go—and slithered away to huddle in the corner with Kel.

In the same burst of movement, Donna materialized beside Joe and took his hand. "We need to dance, you and me," she said. "They've got that guy John McTired spinning tunes."

"What about . . . should we wait?" Joe asked. It wasn't as if he *had* to walk up the stairs with Welk, even though he'd been looking forward to entering the party with him, just for whatever reason you like to walk into a room with someone you think is fun and beautiful and maybe a little bit hot for you.

"Them?" Donna looked over at Kel and Welk, who were murmuring in each other's faces. "You guys? Are you just gonna like crank it right there?"

"We'll be right up," Kel said.

"We'll find you," Welk said.

Joe couldn't even see their faces. "Whatever." He was going to ignore his trippy stomach. "Fuck them, man," he said, tugging on Donna's arm and beginning to climb the stairs. The cigar smokers parted to let them pass, and Joe noticed that their holsters were empty.

"Where's *my* boyfriend, anyway?" Donna said into his ear.

Joe pointed at the ceiling that slanted above them. You could almost see it shake, the music was so loud.

"I said I'll find you!" Welk shouted from the bottom of the stairs. "Shit!"

The storage space was endless and smoky, lighted only by the chandelier that hung from a chain above the dance floor and the flashing pinball machines that were in every corner. Guys leaned into the games with bare, heaving stomachs, and spectators took the occasion to caress. Against one wall there was a makeshift bar, behind which three bartenders danced and passed out beers.

Donna hooked her arm around his waist and they shuffled into the thick of things, the music and the dancers, dropping their feet in time to the heavy beat. When they were close to the center of the dance floor, she let go of him so she could tear it up, so she could shake some funk out of her ass. Ovals and spirals of dance music descended from the ceiling and bounced off the pointy parts of her body. Joe knew that it was just a trick of the synthesizers, but who really cared? The feeling that the music sent through him was reason enough for synthesizers to have been invented. He settled into a thumpy seam. He was oblivious, bending and working his arms as a rueful voice emerged from within the music and kept repeating the same words.

Donna, with her hands waving above her head, drew up beside Joe and bumped her hip against his. And again and again, her head wiggling as if at the end of a springy toy neck. Carved piano notes hung in the air, followed by the thunderclap of drums. Along the outside wall, someone had unlatched all of the French doors—anything to get a breeze. An exterior lamp threw curling shadows across the flapping, peeling doors. Banana-tree leaves poked inside as if they were curious, checking out the party.

Joe didn't think there could be a worthier room anywhere in town—not with this easy crowd, this loud, nimble music, this warm, sweet breeze. He closed his eyes and threw his head back, and for just a moment it was as if he were the singer of a joyful song, overcome by the union of perfect rhythm and rhyme.

When he opened his eyes, he saw Welk galloping sideways across the floor toward him. His hands were in his pockets and his sweaty T-shirt clung to the slope of his chest like a mummy's wrap. It turned Joe's heart inside out to see how tweaked on crystal the boy was—too large for his own head, shoulders and elbows locked.

Don't you know I want to be in love with you?

Even though he was pissed off, he kept his eyes friendly as Welk approached.

"Can I dance over here?" he asked Joe. There was a hole in the shoulder of his T-shirt that Joe wanted to lick. "I'm hearing good things! About our trial, man. Very, very good things."

Joe pretended that the music was so loud he couldn't hear. He closed his eyes again and kept moving.

"Don't be a freak, man," Welk shouted. "I wanna dance here!" Then, more softly: "I want you to tell me I can."

Some people, Joe thought, can get away with anything.

He opened his eyes to find Welk's face just a millionth of an inch from his own. "You can dance here," Joe said.

"That's a start," Welk's sweet mouth said.

With his left hand tight against his hip, Joe beckoned White Donna, who was dancing with Kel. He looked from her face back to Welk, then caught her eye again. He curled his index finger slowly, in the motion of a striking cobra. For a moment, all of the instruments and sound effects in the majestic, wiggy music disappeared, and the diva's voice was all alone.

As the bass and kaboom returned to the speakers, Donna wiggled to Joe's side, slid her arm around his shoulder, and said to his ear, "Joe-Joe? Whatsie?" She kissed the sweaty buzzed hair on the side of his head. "What do you want?"

"I fucking love you," he shouted. "I do. You're so nice to me it makes me want to weep! I'm serious."

"I'm glad," she said. "Thank you. And do you see my boyfriend anywhere?"

"That's the other thing," Joe said, shimmying his crotch against the front of her leg without actually touching her, "I don't think I'm going to want a ride home with you guys. Or whatever."

"Chris will shit."

"Check this out: I totally can't worry about him."

"Whatever," Donna said. But she was smiling.

10:40 p.m.

Now, Seth said to himself, there's going to be hell to pay.

He watched the courtroom from his cramped seat in the jury box. In these moments before the announcement of the verdict, it was noisily filled to standing room with reporters, including three he recognized from the *Times-Picayune*, two from WWL-TV, and a stringer each from *USA Today* and Reuters. Also filling up seats were a half dozen St. Leo the Great parishioners, who prayed voluptuously for the Catholic souls of the Lady Rampart orphans; the youngest of the plaintiff orphans themselves, dressed sweetly in identical Southern-boy suits (khakis and white broadcloth buttondown shirts and blue blazers and tan bucks); the orphans' six fresh-faced lawyers, a mix of pro bono and Legal Aid; Myrtha Shaw; the Shaw Foundation legal team, who were five members of the city's richest firm. And just now making her way to her seat was Rae Schipke, wrapped in a tight, red, leather dress.

Oh, Rae, if only you could have been there, Seth thought; if only you could have seen my spirits rise! Rae, Rae, Rae. You think you know me, but you don't. You don't know what I'm capable of.

Sharp-eyed Judge Robicheaux shouted, "Let's have quiet in the courtroom! Ms. Schipke, may we have your attention?"

"I'm sorry, Your Honor," Rae said contritely and sat down and bowed her head.

The exchange between judge and defendant had an immediate effect on Seth. It engendered the giddy fear that he'd experienced as a child when the roller coaster car crested and he could see the drop before him.

Robicheaux, wiggling his damp beard at the audience, gave a roaring Cajun laugh before saying, "I've instructed the jurors of their rights and responsibilities. Of their roles as citizens. Of the rules of evidence." He caught Seth's eye. "Mr. Foreman, has the jury reached a verdict?"

"Yes, Your Honor," Seth said, "we have."

"Madame Clerk will please note that the jury has reached a verdict."

"Yes, Your Honor."

The rubber-encased T-bar held Seth in the car, teetering here, for a minute, at the pinnacle. There were screams all around him, and the high roaring wind. He sucked in a deep breath and looked across the room at Myrtha Shaw. Certainty and calm emanated from her. He tried to steal some of it from her, his eyes worshiping her as if she were a religious statuette carved from hickory and hanging from a chapel wall. An icon with puckered face and close-trimmed butterscotch hair.

He raised the sealed envelope to shoulder height and

glanced at Rae Schipke. *I owe you, Rae. I hope that you fall with some dignity, and I hope that I never see your face again.*

A chubby court officer ambled to the jury-box railing and lifted the verdict from Seth's hand, carried it to Robicheaux. After the judge read it, he handed it to the court reporter. Without seeming to open her mouth, she read it aloud.

Rae Schipke screamed. The courtroom became a sound studio of exclamations and photo flashes.

1 1 : 3 0   p . m .

A gust of wind blew through the open window beside the bed, slamming the door shut and startling Sherry Keith, Joe's mother, who lay on top of the covers beside a pile of funding-proposal drafts. The hospital that Sherry worked for wanted money to erect a new waiting-room pavilion and a biomedical engineering wing like the one that the LSU Hospital had just built, as well as a dozen smaller projects. For each funding need, there were task forces, consultants, and meetings, endless goddamn meetings. Fund-raising was not the career she'd dreamed of as a girl.

Lovely, Sherry said to herself, and glared at the proposals, all of which required her approval before they could go out in the mail. Their stuck-up prose sickened her, especially because it seemed to be such a perfect evocation of the way the hospital would talk, if it could. *Because I want the———Foundation to continue to be an integral part of the hospital's growth as we enter the twenty-first century, I am asking you to consider funding a capital project with a leadership gift of $[ ] to our present campaign. Enclosed, you will find several projects for your consideration, with commitments ranging from $2 million to $50 million.*

Many of the foundations played games with the hospital, matching it against rivals while having no intention of making a grant. The word among players at the monthly lunch of the National Society of Fund Raising Executives, New Orleans branch, was that certain foundations—the Whitsunday Trust, Discon Foundation, and Fontenot Family Charities, for instance—hadn't made *any* new gifts in at least four years, even though their boards still met regularly and their tax returns showed otherwise. And some foundations—the Kina French Trust, the Myrtha Murphy Shaw Foundation, the Bronte Fund—were tied up in lawsuits. You'd read about the misdeeds in the newspaper and get a raw sickness in your gut, but still you had to kiss the foundation's ass, just in case. Sherry's hospital had current proposals "under consideration" at every trust in town, regardless of their legal status. And that's my job, she always said to herself. Used to be a nurse and then I made myself into something else entirely.

She pushed the proposals to the side of the bed and threw her head back on the stack of pillows and turned on her side. The pillows smelled like peppermint, the lingering charm of one of Joe's goofy all-natural laundry detergents.

Joe, come on, you promised.

She wouldn't be able to go to sleep until he was home. Never had been able to. He had to be shut inside his bedroom. The front and back doors had to be bolt locked. Only then could she doze off—and even then with her door open so she could listen for intruders. She knew where every shadow fell in the dark house at three a.m., and again at six. She recognized the noise of creaking aluminum siding and branches tapping the windows. The only times she couldn't hear the sounds of her house were when the central air-conditioning pump first roared to life in its spot outside her window; after a few minutes, the pump settled into a gentler hum.

With just herself and Joe in the house, there was a different kind of anticipation before she went to sleep. She had only one person to expect home, and in a few years he'd be gone. No more husband, no more son—Sherry, Sherry, what will you do then?

Lately, since Andy's death, she'd been thinking about Florida and her past there and how nice it might be to move back.

They'd been some of the best days of her life, when she was a nurse and Andy was an orderly and they both worked the seven-to-three-thirty shift. Routines, gentle voices, windows open to let in the predawn breeze from the nearby ocean. It had been Sherry's job to make sure that Joe was dressed by five fifty-five. Andy, out in the kitchen, fixed a portable breakfast: banana bread and orange sections and a thermos of coffee and a plastic squirt bottle of apple juice. She'd sneak up behind him, put her cheek against his skinny, suntanned back, pat his butt through washed-out boxers. They ate in the car, still waking up, listening to the radio news. The sun rose from the same pocket of the sky that was blue-black and green like a reflection of the ocean. The old Corvair, gold, with just the lap seat belts, shifted cleanly as it sped across the grated sections of Dania's low-arch drawbridges.

When Andy first got sick, their family doctor couldn't make a diagnosis, so Sherry had to take him from specialist to specialist. She gathered and carried records from hospital to hospital, kept track of his medications, read up on new advances in trade journals whose advertisements for equipment, drugs, and software left her breathless. Right before he died, propped up in bed watching the sun set over the Indian Ocean, he gripped her hand tight and said, "When I married you, I meant for you to have *everything*." His skin was translucent, his eyes sunken in their hollows; he weighed 120 pounds. Sherry hummed the gentlest songs she knew, songs by the Eagles and Linda Rondstadt, as she waited for him to die.

■

On a pillow beside Sherry's head, the phone rang. Half dazed by reverie, she unfolded it and answered, "Joe, no bullshit, where are you?"

"Hello," a woman said brightly. "I apologize for calling so late, but I have an urgent message for Sherry Keith of the Tulane University Medical Center."

She pushed herself upright in bed. "This is Sherry Keith."

"Oh, *good*. Hi, Sherry. It's terrible of me to call this late, and I apologize. I'm calling on behalf of the board of directors of the Shaw Foundation."

"Can we talk about this after the weekend?" Sherry said coldly. "I don't take business calls at this time of night."

"I realize that, and please let me apologize again. I wouldn't call if it weren't urgent."

"Please don't apologize again," she said wearily. "What can I do for you?"

"We've talked before, haven't we?"

"You haven't introduced yourself."

"Oh, I haven't?"

"No."

"My name is Rae Schipke. I'm the executive director at Shaw."

"Ms. Schipke, don't you have some more pressing concerns at the moment? I've been reading about your situation in the paper."

"I have good news for you."

"A grant?" Sherry said before she could stop herself, her voice suddenly and stupidly high pitched. Her face grew hot. *A grant? Put a nice exclamation point on a shitty, shitty summer. My totals are low this quarter.* "A grant would be extraordinary news."

"I wouldn't ever call this late," Rae said in a hushed, confidential voice, "but I wanted to tell . . . you . . . first. I was sure you'd want to know . . ."

"What? What would I want to know, Ms. Schipke?"

"Please call me Rae."

"Rae, it's very late."

"The Shaw Foundation will fund your waiting-room pavilion. We will make two five-million-dollar payments. We liked the plans you submitted, as well as the revised mission statement. The board asks that you name the pavilion for Mrs. Shaw."

Sherry was out of bed, dancing softly around the room. The pavilion was a hard sell, and here she had gone and sold it. She could scarcely believe her ears. "This is tre*men*dous," she said. "Thank you on behalf of the chancellor and on my behalf, too. I don't even know where to begin. This is such a boost to our campaign."

"We respect the staff at Tulane; we all get our doctoring there; wouldn't have it any other way."

"Let me catch my breath. Hoo! There! I'll be very interested to know what Mrs. Shaw thinks of the finished pavilion. We break ground in a month. I'd like to talk to her before we issue the press release. Do you want us to write the release?"

"I think Mrs. Shaw would like to do it herself. I'll ask her."

Sherry made an admiring coo. "What a remarkable woman she is."

There was a sudden dead space on the line, followed by Schipke's booming voice: "Thought you'd appreciate me contacting you first. The Shaws wanted me to talk directly to Chancellor Trilby, but I know the fund-raising world. You've done all the hard work, Sherry—every bit of legwork, I'd guess. You and I will have to build a meaningful partnership. We'll be working closely. Which is why, I guess, I rather arrogantly took the liberty of interrupting you at this late hour. I've been busy this evening, but as soon as I was free I got into the car and I drove right out here—"

"You what?" Sherry stopped in place. She reached for the doorknob and leaned into the doorway, listening. "Where are you?"

"I'm out in the driveway."

"You're in my driveway."

"Yes. I'm here with the check for the first installment. I'd like to present it to you before I take off for a vacation I've planned."

Sherry hesitated a moment—as long as it took for her imagination to create and sign a $5 million check—before saying, "Absolutely. I'm being very ungracious. The chancellor would have my head if he could see me in action."

"Were you asleep? I do apologize, Sherry."

"Just one minute, one minute. Let me have one minute."

"I certainly will. I'm sorry that this is so uncomfortable for you."

"Hold on, Rae. I'm coming." Sherry loped into the hall, pulling her bedroom door shut after her; she had the workday's panties and bras lying on the floor, and what if Schipke asked to use the bathroom and had to walk past the bedroom to get there and looked in and saw what a pig she was?

She was halfway down the hall when she heard just the echo of a gruff voice carried on the wind—as if it came from the back yard. She stopped in place. The hallway was dark, and she hesitated before taking another step to reach the light switch. She thought about going back to her bedroom to see if Schipke was still on the phone, see what was that noise.

What is it?

Nothing; answer the door. It was five million, blowing in the wind.

She did feel safer, just knowing that Joe was due home any minute. He was never more than a half hour late. Funny, wasn't it? He turns sixteen and suddenly she felt certain that she could rely on him. She'd do for him, and he'd do for her.

Her eyes had adjusted to the darkness of the living room ahead of her: familiar shapes, the packages she needed to put away, the sofa, the clock on a table, slowly clicking.

She tripped across the floor and flipped on the overhead light; it was a glass wand that hung low from a silver chain— some stupid design that she'd hated the moment it was installed—and gave the room a flat glow.

She was unlocking the door when she heard a noise that made her scalp tingle: a high-pitched voice, like a small child's. She thought about locking the door again, but her hands didn't listen and she pulled the door open. The screen door—white metal framing a screen that took up half the door—swung shut and latched.

"Rae?" she called.

Nothing, no one—not from where she stood. Just the lawn, smooth as ice cream; the rose bushes climbing the split-rail fence; the mailbox; the tall black-and-chrome driveway light; the few illuminated windows of neighboring houses.

"Hello?" she called in a low voice, unlatching and then propping the screen door open with her shoulder, leaning out into the silent nighttime, the deep black-blue sky spangled with black clouds that poured toward the horizon, as if the earth itself were being pulled out of its place and the sky were coming undone. There was a sharp metal smell in the air. She leaned farther out of the door to see past the trees and shrubs that flanked the front door.

A red minivan sat in the driveway. "Rae?" Sherry called. There was the sound of wings fluttering: moths above her head, beating against the porch light.

And then, smiling, floating directly before her, the face of Rae Schipke, and her thin neck, the whole woman, in a red dress of tight, creased leather. Schipke extended her hand. "Fantastic project, Sherry," she said in a buttery voice. "Congratulations! Let me be the first to congratulate you. May I come in? This will just take one minute."

Sherry had always believed that the most dangerous people were those who wanted "just one minute," and suddenly she had an awful feeling about the woman standing before her. The cold feeling melted from her stomach through her legs and into her feet. "My house is a terrible mess," she said softly. "I'm sorry; I can't invite you in. My son's asleep and I wouldn't want to awaken him."

"I *don't* mean to insist," Rae said, and she grabbed hold of the edge of the screen door and started to pull it toward her.

"Don't you dare!" Sherry pulled hard on the latch, bringing the door toward her. Just as she heard the hard metal click of the latch pin fastening, Rae Schipke's fist punched through the screen. Her hand seized Sherry's and twisted it off the latch.

Schipke laughed in short, airy bursts and pushed her other hand through the same screen hole, bursting it wider, and took a fistful of Sherry's hair, pulling her screaming face up against the screen, and then out through the hole so that the front of her face—all the way to her ears, which were caught on the piercing spokes of wire—was out in the air. All that Sherry could hear was the *thrum thrum* of moths beating against the light.

Schipke pulled the screen door open another few inches, and Sherry fought to pull it back, but the wires dug into her face with every motion. In the alarm-ringing recesses of her brain, she feared decapitation. She cried out and dug her fingertips into the slot where the screen fitted into the door frame. She pulled with a panicked burst of strength and at the same time yanked her head free of the screen. She didn't know she had taken her chain of car and house keys off the table inside the door until she had brought the spiked end of her trunk key into the palm of Schipke's hand.

She lurched back a step and pushed the wood door shut with her shoulder and thigh. It immediately began to bounce inward.

"Shit, shit, shit, shit," she said to herself, fumbling her hand along the side of the door, taking hold of the bolt-lock knob. Her thumb pressed on it.

The door bumped inwards and two fingers wiggled around the side.

She shoulder-butted against the door and slammed the fingers, and they slithered out of sight, and she thumb-and-index-fingered the bolt lock, then hit it with the palm of her hand.

And the door thudded inward against her forehead hard enough to knock her to the floor.

She landed on her back.

Up, she ordered herself.

She twisted onto her hands and knees and tried to push up to her feet.

Up, Sherry, and she rose and stumbled in the dark and, teetering, grabbed hold of the hanging glass light fixture. It came out of the ceiling as she was knocked flying forward into the kitchen. She landed hard on her elbows and chin. Her mouth clamped down on her tongue. The wand light skidded across the floor and shattered against the wall.

The front door slammed shut, and then footsteps ran toward her; knees pressed into the backs of her legs, and her hands were pulled tight behind her.

Schipke's voice: "Where's Joe? Don't make me put you on my list."

"What do you—?"

"Tell me," Schipke said, "where's your little son?"

11:30 p.m.

Seth waited in standstill traffic to get on the highway. His Toyota sat on a road beneath a road; fitting, he thought: a wet road twinkling with broken glass and glamorized with stunted palm trees and abandoned grocery carts. The massive highway supports on either side of him lent a fucked-up aspect to the setting. Was he inside or was he outside? There was a roof, there were walls. But however you called it, you were in a dark-as-shit place. The only illumination came from headlights and the sparkling floats of the passing festival parade. It was the last of the evening.

Seth was first in line, but his access to the on-ramp was blocked by three police cars a few yards in front of him. Extending from the police barricade all along the parade route as far as he could see were flimsy metal fences that nominally separated the parade from the crowds of revelers ten or fifteen deep. The throngs were everywhere, even pressed up against Seth's newish green sedan. They were looking in at him, just teeth and eyes in the dark.

Can I withstand their fucking gaze? he asked himself.

I can.

But how much longer for this parade? The floats were wood-and-papier-mâché representations of sea nymphs and tortoises and plump ruby fish. Girls in bikinis with their skin painted pink clapped in time to the music as they strutted on runways along the edge of the spotlighted float that was on view now. It was some kind of trippy lair—perhaps the home of an eel, Seth thought, an eel with a tired psychedelic interest in home decor. The girls were either eels or eel feed; the latter, he hoped desultorily.

He wished he had a cigarette and a beer and a sixty-four-ounce frozen daiquiri, one of the hundred-proof brands sold by the storefronts on Bourbon, and a bottle or two of Xanax or Valium, something mellow to grind up and snort. To get the jump on this town, he had to stay cool.

He looked away from the float, fixed his gaze on the comforting lights of his dash. They were complemented by the spangle of shadows and colors thrown off by the eel lair. If these strobes and flashes didn't stop soon, he thought he might cry.

The car phone shrilled.

Then a second time.

He looked down at it with mild affection and tore it from its cradle. "Yeah?" he said.

No answer.

Then: "*Oh, hi.*"

"Can you talk, sweetie?"

"Maybe it's not a good time."

"They showed you on CNN. Your father and I worry."

"I don't think it's a good time to talk."

"We're ready to talk to you, Seth. We want to sit down with you and work things out."

"*Mom.* I want to do that, too. But, Mom, we can't talk right now."

"Honey, there's music. Are you near a bar?"

"Mom, I'm going to hang up."

"Will you call me? What more can we do? We have both looked deep in our hearts. We were never perfect. We never said we were. Why can't you give it another chance?"

"I'll call you. Mom, I'll call, but it's not gonna be real soon. There's some changes in my life."

"Why? Let me put your father on."

"Mom, don't get yourselves upset over me. There's better things to worry about. Good night." He hung up.

He thought to himself, Yes, yes, I'm ready to haul ass with just a quick stop at my apartment, lah-de-dah, but where in the fuck am I gonna go? Am I gonna take a chance on Mobile? On Dothen? Destin? He had a friend in Why, Arizona, right on the Mexican border. He had some friends in New York and one in Lancaster, Pennsylvania—what was her name, Thelma?

He was going to miss his New Orleans. He ached sometimes when he left town on business. Late summer here, nothing like it anywhere. The wet tent of final summer nights hung over you, and as much as you longed for relief, part of you was sad that its fierceness had to end.

The phone rang again. The digital beep hung in the air like a knife-movie scream; you'd heard the same shriek before, but it still fucked with your head. Just as he decided to let the machine pick up, and settled in his seat, a scrawny man pressed his pale, greasy chest against the driver's side window. He writhed against the glass, leaving a milky smear.

Unperturbed, Seth leaned across the passenger seat and fumbled in the glove compartment for his gun. "Hey, belly dancer," he said through the opening at the top of the window, "pass by." When he pointed the gun through the opening, the man and his belly disappeared.

The phone stopped ringing.

A new float passed in front of him. On this one, a sea dragon's mouth slowly opened and closed; inside the mouth, spotlighted in blue among the pointy teeth, were three children who danced across the rubbery tongue and threw strings of plastic beads to the crowd. In the sea dragon's nostrils and eye sockets, more children threw plastic. The float gleamed with hard fiberglassiness.

The phone rang again, and this time Seth picked up on the first ring. "Yeah?"

"We just watched you on television," said Rae Schipke, and the temperature of Seth's heart dropped fifty degrees. "Wait, can I put you on hold for a minute?"

"I'm not going anywhere," he said steadily.

"That's right. You might try, but you're *not* going anywhere."

The line went cold. Schipke's airy self-control filled Seth with dread. Of course she was jacked off, but you couldn't tell from her voice. She had that expertise of demeanor, like famous people. When she gave one of her nauseating motivational lectures to reporters or foundation supplicants, love of the moment seeped from her pores. She'd picked up mannerisms from Diane Sawyer, of course, and Lynne Cheney, and Sharon Stone, and smaller portions of John Sununu and Bruce Willis. Which was not to say that the hard core of her own personality didn't radiate clearly through the borrowed material.

The phone whirred and crackled and then Rae Schipke came on the line: "Hi, I'm back. Just watched you on TV."

"So you told me."

"Well, you looked gorgeous and robust."

"Thanks."

"Let me tell you what the downside is."

"What's the downside?"

"I'm glad you asked."

"On TV, you look brawny and capable, but you also look like the piece of shit you are." Rae was quiet for a moment, and then she said, "You *fucked* me."

"Yeah," Seth mumbled. "Can't deny it."

"How did you *think* that you'd get away with *fucking* me? I'm going to bite a hole in your cheek and suck your brains out. You have *never* had reason to feel the kind of fear you should feel now."

"Rae . . ."

"Don't interrupt me and don't hang up on me. What's that noise I hear?"

"It's a parade."

"You're on St. Charles? I'm writing that down, mother-fucker. You're on my list."

"I could be on St. Charles. I could be in Metairie. I could be in Algiers. There's parades everywhere."

"How's the crowd? Are the blacks happy? That's all I fucking care about. I don't sleep nights if I think the black people aren't pacified."

"Jesus, Rae. Be quiet for a second. You're giving me a fistula."

"Get a fucking proctologist," she began, and then tore off on another run of invective.

He held the phone away from his ear while she went on.

She was not going to calm down. She was not going to *work it out of her system.* Rae's system had been soldered shut a long time ago by master mechanics; everything that was *in* her engine was going to *stay* in her engine: ice, then water, then steam, then condensation, without a molecule escaping.

The parade was coming close to its end. Hooded black guys holding torches passed in the wake of a funky high school marching band whose percussion regiment danced in dips and back steps. The music was enormous; it glimmered from the instruments and crashed over the top of Seth's car. He experienced a few shudders of ecstasy. His eyes welled up as he imagined himself abandoning the Toyota and joining the parade, leaving behind his car for the police to impound and then rip apart and test for signs of his murder.

"Okay, okay," he said into the phone, settling it back into place along the side of his face.

". . . and the faggots and the hobo white niggers and the *chicas* and all the rest of them? Are they all drunk and kissy and *occupés* with the spectacle? I put them all on my list."

"My ass is bleeding, Rae. I'm sorry, but you're going to have to stop riding me. Lower your voice."

"I need to see you."

"I'm sorry."

"Seth, come talk to me baby. I have something for you."

"I have plans."

"You do?"

"I'm disappearing."

"You have no idea. You have just sewn up quite a verdict against Rae Schipke. A judgment of twenty-five million dollars against the Shaw Foundation. Is that cute? Your shit is green and pulpy and all over my face, bitch."

"Goodbye, Rae."

"Is the boy with you?"

Seth gazed blankly out the window. One of the last floats, the length of two eighteen-wheelers, passed. Grass-skirted muscle men waved frantically from their perches. "I don't know what you're talking about."

"The boy. You introduced us at the health club."

The clock of his memory spun backwards in a rush. For a moment, he couldn't remember anything before the trial, the sequestration, the verdict. Then, projected against the red screen inside his eyelids, he saw the boy in the alcove beside the pool. A nice morsel. A little *male* for his taste, but he'd always allowed himself the occasional lapse. "That boy? Him? Are we talking about the same boy?"

"Yes him. Joe Keith."

"What does he have to do with you? Rae, he couldn't be more inconsequential to me."

Mellow laughter floated from the phone. "This ain't standard operating procedure, is it darling? We haven't grown this relationship successfully, have we? From the start, it's been cross-purposes and competition."

"Goodbye, Rae. Just for the record, I think you got what you deserved."

"Just one more thing." The phone went dead for a moment, and then there was the sound of wheezing gasps and thin whimpers.

The sound made Seth's chest constrict. He closed his eyes. "What's that?"

"A friend."

"Who's that, Rae?"

"I came looking for the boy. This is who I found. I'm with his mother." After a short pause, she said, "You took my life away from me. Like *that*, I'm gonna get the balance right."

Seth was quiet.

"I have eyes," she said gruffly.

"I don't dispute it."

"I saw the look in your eye when you came out from fucking him in that little dark space beside the pool. The both of you dripping wet."

"*Rae*, that's not what happened. I didn't make a loving bond, if that's what you're thinking. I have not thought of that kid even once. You've made a tremendous, insane mistake. Get *away* from those people. Leave them alone. I know that you're a bad enough bitch to kill. With your back against the wall, you'd kill. If your life or money were at risk, you'd hurt, maim. But do you have the kind of steel fucking stupid fury to hunt down and revenge-kill a random innocent boy? Or his *mother?*"

"No. No, no, no. Don't put this back on me."

"It's *on* you, Rae. It's *all* on you."

"I'm disappearing tonight. Poof! And I will leave my mark on you. I will!" Her voice dwindled away in static.

"Rae. If you want to disappear, just *go.*"

She buzzed back on the line. "If you suffered an attack of shame and conscience in the jury room, that's one thing. *One* thing. There are rules in the world, and one of them is that the innocent will suffer. In this life, I've had to take whatever opportunities I could. Now, okay, I'm going to offer you an address. If you don't come to me, or if you shamefully call the police, then it won't be only me and you who disappear."

"What are you doing, Rae? Rae."

"Get a pen," she said. "Here's the address."

■

White girls in high-cut leotards danced across the Rock 100 float, four enormous speakers connected by catwalks. The whole thing was done up as a barnacle-encrusted pirate's chest full of cheerful booty. Seth looked away from the girls to the tail end of the parade, straggling hooded black men dragging their torches. The spectators were dwindling away—blacks and whites, idiots and drunks and families and lovers and weaklings. All of them, all of *you*, Seth thought, oblivious to the times and to the fate of their city. It was late in the century for people to pretend they were safe in their revelry on the stinking streets.

I resign, he said to himself. I'm sinking down into the mire. *Glub glub glub.*

He turned on the radio, twisted the dial until he found white noise. He closed his eyes.

He had done a hundred bad things, a thousand, ten million. Why stop there? He had taken careful part in an infinite amount of wrongdoing. But only once had he almost killed someone. And it was a stain that he could never—not with any amount of penance—erase. He had been filled with intent. He had been a monster, and he could be one again—any old time.

He saw himself sprinting across the front of the Tulane campus on a dripping June night. Light spilled from posts, making small pools, but most of the grounds were dark canopies of linden leaves and brush-top palms and droops of willow branches above meandering lawns and puddled macadam walkways. There was a dead quiet.

The campus was cut in half by Freret Street. He crossed, at a crouching pace, and picked up speed, bounding across the lawn of brick-and-glass Woldenburg Hall, up the overspilling apron of steps. He used a stolen access card to get into the building. The glass door locked behind him.

His breath hung in his ears. *Hhuh, hhuh, hhuh.* He stood noiseless in the marble lobby, gathered himself, pulled a nylon runner's hood over his face, and then padded down the hall of locked doors to the offices of the Citizen Law Clinic.

Dim light showed beneath the door. Seth listened for a minute. Silence. He knocked.

"Hello?" called the voice inside.

Seth didn't answer. *Was it the right guy?*

"Who is it?" the voice called.

Seth smiled. *Yes.* It was Jim Yonce, with his suit against the Shaw Foundation, his loud talk. Rae Schipke wanted a scare put in him, and Seth wanted—he really wanted—to prove his mettle.

He knocked on the door again and shouted, "Physical plant!"

Yonce was yawning when he opened the door. His hair was pressed to the side of his head; he'd been asleep. Behind him, a desk was covered with file folders and two blazing lamps. The blinds were down. His smile crumpled as he tried to close the door.

"I don't think so," Seth said. He lifted the knotted bunch of thin wires over his head and shouldered his way into the room. He kicked the door shut behind him. There was one millisecond when he thought he might turn around, but it passed.

"No, no, don't," whimpered Yonce, trying to cover his face with his hands.

He was a picture of powerlessness. The *man.* Advocate, doing good on behalf of the community.

"Your time has passed, man," Seth said, and he brought the wires down across Yonce's legs.

Yonce fell to the floor.

The wires slit his T-shirt so ribbons of blood soaked the fabric. They tore into his face, the tip of his tongue, the open mouth trying to call for help.

"Desist!" Seth shouted.

Yonce didn't move, and Seth kicked him in the ribs, brought the wires down again. He was lost in his fury.

Now, horns beeped around his car. He jolted upright in his seat, fixed his eyes on the clear space in front of him, and accelerated between the parting police cars. He turned left, zoomed up the highway ramp. All that he could see through the sinuous curve of his windshield were the beams and moons of headlights and the sky that was full of dark, pitted clouds. He could still hear the music of the parade, but he didn't know where, in relation to his car, it was. He laid on his horn and sped into the mess of traffic heading out of the city.

12:45 a.m.

Rampart Street was the far frontier of the Quarter. In the first block off Canal, you could entertain the illusion that you were protected by the private police who watched over the crowds milling around the cavernous Saenger Theater, all lighted up for a show, and the New Orleans Athletic Center, dark for the night except for its adjoining garage, but the farther away from Canal that you traveled, the emptier and wilder Rampart became. One block after the next was made up of empty parking lots littered with hubcaps and windshield glass; ramshackle, boarded-up, ice-creamy houses; pithole, hard-luck bars blasting old Journey songs and the stench of stale whiskey sours and sweet metallic smoke. Across the street from the strip of bars was a cemetery fortress, high gates surrounding aboveground crypts.

Joe and Welk, arms around each other's necks, stood at the

far end of the street, where it intersected with Esplanade, looking up at the red sky.

"We'll see, we'll see," Welk said.

"I'm gonna be so fried," Joe said. "I'm so late."

"Do I have to say it? I don't wanna say it." Welk was using his deep voice; Joe could feel it in rumbles along his rib cage. "I'm gonna be all embarrassed if I come right out . . . and say it . . . and you say you don't wanna."

"I wanna. You don't *have* to say stuff. We can just like stand here." To have Welk hanging on him, anchoring him to the spot, was a perfect kind of burden.

"We don't need to be out here on the street, dude, all messed up."

"*I'm* not messed up."

"Pipe down, pipe down."

"What's that up there?" Joe pointed to a misshapen blob that was parked along the curb in the next block. It looked like a car that had melted down, some funky prototype without wheels.

"Let's check it out."

"Whatever."

"Do you want me to find you a fucking cab, man?"

"I guess I kinda should go home."

"Cool. You'll go home. Just come with me to check that thing out. How's that? We'll be almost to my place, and I'll get you a cab."

After a moment, Joe said, "Okay."

They detached from each other and began walking in silence. So this is how it's going to end, Joe thought. My big deal night. Sweet. Even as disappointment welled up in his back and sinus cavities, Joe was also experiencing giddy relief, and the thought of lying in his bed at home took its soothing place in his heart. Tomorrow, he'd get his mom to drive somewhere out in the country, maybe Mississippi, that quarry out-side Picayune, and they'd swim and shoot photos and find a fish fry.

Joe watched Welk out of the corner of his eye. The guy had a *gait*. It was slouchy, but because he was put together so strong, his indifferent posture came off as predatory and wanton. He was slightly bow-legged, maybe perfectly so, and his tense, red-brown, freckled arms chugged along in rhythm like casual pistons.

"I see you looking at me." Welk laughed, high pitched and friendly and surprised.

"I got something in my eye."

"Yeah: *me*."

"Arrogant sumbitches are a blight on me, ding."

"You like to look at me?"

"Chill, special dude."

" 'Cause I like to look at you."

"Yeah, yeah, yeah."

"I keep getting a picture in my head."

"I bet you do, many kinds."

"Of me and you, fucking."

"Har-dee-har."

Welk threw on his brakes and lunged at Joe, caught his head in the crook of his elbow, and pulled Joe's head against his chest. "Har-har," he said. "Listen to how fast my heart's beating, man. Listen to that."

Joe's cheek was tight against the rise of Welk's chest; his chin was in the hollow just below. "I hear it," he said.

"That's 'cause of being with you."

"Or the white powder."

"Not the powder. I had a *taste*." He let go of Joe and started to jog away.

"Hey, I didn't mean to be all grindy," Joe said, following.

Welk, not answering, picked up speed, and then stopped on a dime in front of the mysterious, blobby vehicle.

Joe came up behind him. "A float."

"I don't want to know how that happened to this." Welk tapped the hulk of painted wood and fiberglass with his toe. "I think it was supposed to be a whale. Cut off at the fins."

Joe bent toward it, hunching on the edge of the curb. He touched one of the teeth, which was hard and cold like a real tooth, but painted gray and flaking. He slipped forward, petting the red, furrowed tongue, which was made of plastic. With just a nudge, the tongue sunk on hinges and then popped back into place. He rubbed his hand on the rough inside of the cheek, crawling farther, hand over hand until he was completely inside.

"Hey, Gepetto," Welk said, "don't let the leviathan devour you, dude."

Joe stretched out on the tongue, which bobbled up and down. "I'm getting sleepy, so sleepy. I can feel the juices breaking down my skin. I'm starting to lose consciousness." His voice disappeared out the other, raggedly torn end of the wreckage.

"Is there room for me?"

"There's definitely."

"Can I?"

"Enter the beast, sir, with caution and respect."

"I shall." The outer shell began to shake as Welk climbed in. He bounced on top of the tongue and slid up Joe's body until his face was beside Joe's. "Kiss me."

Joe obliged, and as he explored the inside of Welk's mouth he settled into the lull of the whale's tongue movement, which Welk, by laying his own upper body on top of Joe's and kicking a foot against the inside hull, controlled. Welk's fingers were intertwined with Joe's, and bending Joe's in a backward arc over the edge of the plastic tongue.

"What?" Welk said, pulling his mouth away.

"Let's go," Joe said, trying to hold his smile shut so he didn't actually devour Welk's whole amazing face.

"Where?"

"To you know where."

■

The Sanctuary of Lady Rampart filled a square block on the river side of Rampart, two blocks past the float debris. The front was barren of plants or trees, and the only sign of identification was a small silver plaque embedded in the brick facade: THE MYRTHA SHAW WING, it said in demure lettering. A wide sweep of cement steps led to barred double doors, each of which had a globe-sized pane of dark, stained glass in its center. The main structure was four stories, but there were shorter, more modern additions on either side, absorbed into the main structure by a similarity of window: dozens of skinny barred windows about the height of surfboards, most of them dark, but a few glowing with electric candles.

"We have to go in the back," Welk said. "I kind of missed my curfew. If I ring, the sentry'll have to sign me in, and I don't know which one it is. We'll sink."

"Fine. But if we can't do this easy, I don't know. I'm so late, when I get home it's not even going to be funny."

"Your mom's going to—"

"Don't even go there, dude. I don't even wanna think about it. That's gonna make me totally rank. Just don't say another word about it."

Welk put his hand on Joe's mouth. "Point taken, sir. Back here."

He led down a narrow path beside the building. On the left was a fence overgrown with tall, scratchy stalks; on the right, black windows. At the end of the path there was a brick patio illuminated by bright spotlights, two yellow and one white. Once they rounded the back corner, Welk pointed his jaw at a wall of leaves interwoven with sugary strands of spider webs that topped off just beneath the crumbling white curve of an archway. Beyond the leaves was a dark opening in the facade of the building.

"Through that shit?" Joe asked.

"Shhh." Welk nodded before whispering, "It's the old slaves' quarters."

"*Nasty.*" Joe held his breath and followed into the bristly wet growth. To his surprise, it wasn't as thick as he'd feared, and with no scratches or gooey swipes on his face or arms he was on the other side, in a tiny alcove before a barred door.

"Okay," Welk whispered, and with his hand outstretched like Spiderman's, pressed the pads of his fingertips against one of the door's panes of glass and removed it from its frame. He handed the pane to Joe, touched Joe's earlobe, and then stuck his hand through the hole and unlocked the door.

They entered on a black-and-white tile foyer. Even though a breeze fluttered by from somewhere within, the air in the foyer was heavy and wetly dusty. Welk closed and locked the door and replaced the pane, and then he led down a narrow corridor with fifteen-foot ceilings. After taking a series of abrupt turns, they came upon massive double doors covered with rusted hinges and buckles.

"Let me think for a minute," Welk said, holding up his index finger.

Joe nodded and looked around. The only light came from bare light bulbs that dangled from the ceiling on long wires.

There were three bulbs; the middle one was dark. Joe exhaled loudly and leaped for it, his hand flattened into a paddle. He missed, and landed hard on his ankle.

Welk gave a smart-ass twist of his mouth and crossed his arms over his chest.

Joe crouched, pressing his butt to the wall, and then pushed off and leaped. His hand swiped the wire just above the metal collar of the bulb, and he thought he got a tiny shock. He slid down the wall, resting his haunches on the back of his sneakers, and looked up at the dark bulb reprovingly.

Welk mouthed the word "watch," pointing to his chest, and in a graceful leap hit the bulb with his hand and set it in motion, as Joe had wanted to.

The bulb swung at the end of its wire like a trapeze artist; the momentum of the swing gave it a little hop before it changed direction, as if it were about to somersault to the next wire. After two full swings, it had subtly changed its arc of movement so that it was headed directly for one of the lighted bulbs. Joe braced himself for an explosion, but it didn't happen; instead, the glowing bulb began to swing too, in time with the dark one.

Welk leaned into the doors and pushed them open. "Okay, if I'm right, no one should be able to hear us," he said, stepping into the narrow courtyard. Taking up most of the space was a lap pool with one black racing stripe painted down the center. A couple of dozen potted palms bordered the pool. "This swankness is, of course, courtesy of the Shaw Foundation." Looking down at the water, he cleared his throat violently and spit.

"Nice people."

"I think I'll find out the verdict soon. Somebody should

have left a note on my door. I don't *hear* any celebrating, though."

Joe pulled the doors shut behind him. "Is it all boys that live here?"

"Yep."

"That's what I guess would be uncool. I like being around girls. I like the whole way they have about them. I like seeing 'em move."

"And you don't like watching boys move?"

"Um . . ."

"What's the problem, man? You don't like to look at me?"

"I do. Well, sometimes I get the feeling that I'm maybe like stepping into this whole world of guys who don't ever hang out with girls, like that's what I have to look forward to. And I don't look forward to that."

Welk plucked at the bottom of his T-shirt so the neck stretched down. "Shut it *down*, man. You don't have to *enter* any world or anything. I mean, you might want to visit it or something if you want to meet people. But I mean, stop the bullshit talk. You are not right here with a girl. I'm not a girl, Joe. You're not coming up to some girl's bedroom. But you know what? I've been thinking about you since this afternoon with more like intensity than I bet any girl has ever thought about you. Okay? I haven't been able to *eat* tonight because every time I maybe wanted to I could only think about you and how sick to my stomach I was to get with you and kiss you and shit."

"You put it that way," Joe said, putting his hands on his stomach and wiggling at the knees, "and I feel like I'm actually in a dream. I mean, I can't believe someone would think about me like that."

"I do."

Welk was a resident advisor, so he had a single room at the end of a wide green hall lit by electric candles. The wood-plank floor creaked as he rocked in place outside the door, eyes sparkling with tears. He held a piece of paper that had been thumbtacked to the door; in dark Magic Marker letters, it said: VICTORY, PART ONE. TWENTY-FIVE MILLION. COME DOWNSTAIRS IN THE MORNING, WE'LL TELL YOU ALL ABOUT IT. DON'T WAKE US, BRO. WHERE ARE YOU? The note was signed KEVIN.

"Do you want me to leave, man?" Joe asked. "Maybe you want to see if anyone's awake?"

"I want to celebrate," Welk said, "but my boys are asleep." He gave Joe a fake look of befuddlement. "Hmmm, who could I like celebrate with?"

"Who's Kevin? Is he one of the guys who was with you at So-So's this afternoon?"

"Yeah."

"Was he the blond guy?"

"Yeah."

"Okay."

"Don't go there, dude. Nothing to say. He's my best friend. Him and me were both born in Jackson." With a shove of his shoulder, Welk opened the door to his room. "Enter, sir," he said reverently.

Joe walked past him into the humid darkness, stopping after a couple of steps. Welk bumped against him, pushing him another few steps, and flicked a switch that made four or five table lamps come to life in a corner of the floor. The walls were painted white; the floor was the same wood plank as the hall, but mostly covered with a blue-and-red oriental carpet.

There was a table against the big window in the back of the room; on it, a slick, hefty boom box and piles of tapes. In the center of the floor, two futons were side by side. Joe eyed them with a mix of zeal and alarm. And that was it for furnishings. An alcove off to the side looked like some sort of dressing room, and it led to the bathroom, whose whiteness Joe could see through the open door.

Welk crossed the room and stood in front of the window, which looked out over the pool courtyard: lights reflected in water and shimmering in white arcs and bubbles on the courtyard's brick wall, the brushy tops of banana trees swaying in the wind, the peach and orange and blue starry sky.

"People don't really wear tight jeans any more," Joe said, "but you totally get away with it."

"Peckerman." Welk laughed. "Are these really tight?"

"I don't think I'm imagining it, dude."

"Maybe you're just concentrating too hard."

"Hmmm."

Welk punched a few buttons on the boom box. A silvery, thick rhythm line floated out of the speakers, and after a few seconds a man with a casual, deep voice began to sing a Hendrix cover.

"Who the fuck is this?" Joe asked.

"Give it a chance."

"That's not likely."

"Do you ever just *chill?*"

Joe looked at the bed. "I'm *nervous*," he muttered.

Welk turned to look out the window. "I know. Your hands have been shaking since we came in the room. It's, I don't know, I can say this, I think it's kind of a turn-on."

"Right. My hands haven't been shaking."

Welk didn't answer. Still looking out the window, he lifted one arm up over his shoulder and took a handful of the back of his T-shirt. The muscles in his arm shifted in a way that made Joe almost stagger backward a step or two. Then, with just the one hand, Welk pulled the T-shirt off.

"You're beautiful, man," Joe said quietly, almost to himself, looking at Welk's suntanned back. It had everything going for it: the cleft, the heft, the wing muscles, the *V*-ness. "Holy shit."

"It's just the way I *look*—huh? It doesn't mean that much."

"It means pretty much to me."

"But that's 'cause I want to be with you so bad and I'd be the first person you're with."

"You don't really know that you'd be the first person."

"I'd bet on it."

"So."

Welk turned around now, showing all the amazingly whittled distortions of his chest and his stomach and his shoulders. "I have *eyes*."

"Welk," Joe said, "I have to piss."

"Go," Welk said, gesturing to the dark alcove.

Reluctantly pulling his eyes off him, Joe trudged into the bathroom. He shut the door behind him, found the light and flicked it on, and listened to his breath huffing in his ear. *Hhuh, hhuh, hhuh.* His heart clobbered his ribs at a rate of two or three hundred beats per minute. "Stupid fuck," he said to himself with a bark, and then he pulled off his T-shirt and looked in the medicine cabinet mirror at the stupid fucking body of his. About the same form and appeal as Gumby's hulking physique. And a blank, random Tater Tot face.

Nice.

Hot.

A real deathly attraction.

And what about those suave moves? he asked himself. They are showing some manliness to be sure, Joe Keith.

He unfastened his shorts, pinched their waist and his boxers' waist and slid them down his legs and stepped out of them. He toed them against the wall, where they looked pitifully little boyish.

Still wearing his Pumas, he stepped up to the toilet. He lifted up the lid, the seat. There were two curls of hair stuck to the rim. He took his dick in his hand.

It had always seemed to be normal enough. It wasn't exactly *big* . . .

He closed his eyes for a moment, getting comfortable; when he opened them, his piss started, an arc drilling noisily into the old bowl, which had the acoustics of an amphitheater. The water frothed and foamed clear bubbles.

Knock knock knock.

The door flew open.

"Hey," Welk said, and suddenly he was beside Joe, pissing too. "I couldn't hold it in." His eyes met Joe's. "You look good naked. We're going to have a swell time." He dropped his voice to a whisper: "I know some tricks."

"Like what?" Joe said, shaking off his dick even as it hardened in his hand. He looked down at it, just to make sure it was achieving a decent size.

Welk's piss continued. He had two veins and curly dark hair running from his dick to his belly. "Well," he said, "when I get done, I'm gonna mash my lips all over you, and like hold your dick and my dick in my hand and like rub them and pick you up, dude, and haul you out there to my bed, and we'll"—his stream started to dwindle—"we'll *talk*, about cars, and we'll look at, um, family pictures, and arm wrestle, and I'll beat you, and I'll get to take my prize whichever way I want to. Okay"—he fiddled with it—"I'm done pissing."

"Yeah," Joe said, watching Welk's dick turn red and get hard. "You've got a wicked left hook on that thing, huh?"

Welk lay with his belly between Joe's legs, kissing his neck, biting down gently on the bony muscles. His fingers pressed into the spaces between Joe's ribs. His chest hugged on top of Joe's, holding him against the futon. And Joe let out small, delighted cries, squirming a little bit, barely lifting up his head and looking down on the top of Welk's head, along the back, down the straining hairy legs that fanned out with muscle, and at his own idiot feet, still trapped in fat sneakers that made his ankles look even skinnier than they were.

Unsmacking his mouth from Joe's neck, Welk slid himself a half foot farther up and pressed his forehead to Joe's; with just the least bit of pressure, he pushed the back of Joe's head to the futon. "Hey," he huffed, "how much fun is this?"

"Much," Joe laughed.

"I don't think I have any rubbers."

"Oh."

"What can I do, man?"

"Um . . . it doesn't have to stick in a hole?"

"You know what I like want to do?"

"Yeah?"

"So . . . ?" Welk propped his elbow tight against the side of Joe's face, and molded his forearm across Joe's forehead. "I *really* want to."

"No way," Joe sighed. "Absolutely not. Improvise, man. Do whatever, except, you know, don't do *that*."

"Oh, fuck; you're right." He slid his forearm off Joe's forehead, and they resumed kissing.

Joe's heart was fat with glee.

1 : 0 5 a . m .

On the radio, callers to the *Ear of New Orleans* show on WSOL-AM praised the jury for the righteous hugeness of its award to the orphanage. "Ripped out my heart, those kids," a woman sobbed. "If anyone thinks it was too much money, they're made of granite. I am so *angry* at that woman. I am so *upset.*" The call-in host offered solace, shaded his voice so it matched the incoming wall of theme music, and then, when the music ended, read an advertisement for a personal-injury law firm. Seth clicked the radio off.

He was parked against a boxy wall of shrubbery, just around the corner from Joe's house. He wasn't surprised by the neighborhood, which was modest but brimming with the best luxuries: quietness, darkness, stillness. It suited Joe. The boy hadn't come off as one of those wireless New Orleans millionaire boys whom you'd run into up at the capital or at the racetrack or at Commander's for Sunday brunch, and he wasn't tough like a Bywater yat. He was a Metairie kid.

The houses around here probably topped out at $150,000, so it was unlikely that the residents paid for a private security force. Some of them probably had alarms, and perhaps an off-duty cop made freelance run-throughs twice or three times a night. Otherwise, Seth figured, he was on his own.

He pulled his gun off the passenger seat, cupped it in his palm. Without any great intentions, this was the man he'd become. In the dark, looking for opportunity. Even now, working on what he guessed he could call the side of *good*, he was the same mean fucker; maybe that's what it would take to resolve this situation. The same stealth and readiness, the ability to keep his pulse in check.

But in the back of his mind was the same little worry that had been there when he did jobs for the foundation; it was a mocking, slithery voice telling him that he was going to screw things up.

You're gonna spot your panties, Seth.

You're not fooling anybody, baby.

He popped the car door open and stepped onto the gravelly roadside. He slowly squatted out two deep-knee bends, clicked the door carefully shut, but left it unlocked in case he had to hurry on the return. Stepping around the shrub wall, he took a hard look at the boy's lawn, in which no alarm-system sign was spiked, and at Schipke's van, bathed in light from a driveway lamppost.

Schipke wasn't going anywhere.

The thought struck him cold in the pit of his chest. He wished that he was wrong. If Rae had a plan, if she had an orderly agenda, then she'd know that her clock was ticking and she had only limited time to escape. But she shouldn't be in a house on this quiet street. She shouldn't have visited herself on this neighborhood. There was no telling what she would do. She could fall apart, give herself up, or she could shoot the mother and then herself. For all Seth knew, she had the boy with her, too, and was simply waiting.

What room are you in, Rae? Where are you? What have you done?

He drew back his shoulders and sucked in a breath, let it out, and then he set off, running across one lawn into the next, into the shadows beside the boy's house. Dew lifted off the grass, clinging to his ankles. His breath came easily. His thoughts were clear as he made his way into the back yard.

His eyes adjusted and he took in the contours of a well-tended garden: benches and potted trees, flower beds, a stone pathway. He was reminded again that home and family were the sneakiest motherfuckers in any fight: come up on you, they would, hands all gripped tight on your heart, making you cry, give up. He didn't want to be here, where these people had lavished so much care. He'd already run away from one mom.

He stepped backward, one slow step over the other, into the garden to get a wide-angle view of the back of the house. Windows and a set of French doors. Lights on in what was probably the largest bedroom, and in the kitchen. Between the lighted windows there was one dark: a small bathroom window, he guessed. He stepped up onto one of the stone benches for a moment so he could see into the kitchen window; then he dropped back to the grass. He didn't know what to make of the scene he saw: both women sat hunched at a table, heads together; they could have been old college friends. There was no gun in sight, no ropes, leather hoods, or scythes.

You don't know how to do the dirty work, Rae. You always had someone else do it for you. Why don't you run, girl, just run on down to Brazil.

There was a rustle of grass behind him, and before he could turn to see its source, a rabbit ran between his legs. It hopped twice and disappeared around the side of the house. Seth sucked in a laugh and then returned his attention to the house.

He was choosing among the windows, deciding which one would be the easiest and quietest to open, when his eye settled on a dark stripe between the two French doors; they were slightly ajar. With two dozen steps, he was just outside the doors, looking through one clean pane sideways into the kitchen. The table was now empty. He shifted his sight straight ahead, into the dark dining room, making sure that Rae wasn't hidden in any of the shadows.

He tapped his fingertips against the pane of glass beside the outer doorknob, and the door spilled slightly inward. With a second bump, it made a creak just loud enough for his gut to drop, but now it was open wide enough for him to step inside. Okay, he said to himself, pulling his second leg inside. Okay, okay, gun up, gun pointing ahead, you can guess exactly where you are. Step-slide around the table, big mother; step, step, quiet, quiet now; okay, watch the chair legs, gun up, finger poised; steady, keep it together, okay.

He ran his eyes over bags and boxes and piles and clothes draped on furniture in the dark living room. He stood motionless, listening to the blood thud along his jawline, in his temples. He made an inventory of the floor ahead of him, looking for a clear path. Go, he told himself. Go. He heard a hitch in his hipbone as he took a step forward, but the sound of his shoe breaking glass was the last thing he heard before the living room lights—lamps on tables at each end of the sofa, sparks snowing from the wires of a hanging fixture—blazed to life. He looked instinctively at his foot, and the twisted pair of eyeglasses beneath his shoe, and then he looked up at Rae Schipke. A bullet whizzed past his face and landed with a solid thud in the wall over his right shoulder. He cringed, and his gun slipped down his fingers as if a prop in a magic show. He watched it clatter to the floor.

This is some shit, Seth; you're quite the operator.

It suddenly occurred to him that he'd never faced an armed opponent.

"Don't you know how to shut a door?" Rae asked, approaching with a *clip clap* drag of her shoes on the wood floor. "Do you have someone with you?"

"I don't plan on staying," he said, and then blurted, "Hey, you missed me. Does that mean something? C'mon, Rae, look at me for a second."

She righted her chin and met his eyes. Hers glittered. "What could it mean?"

"You don't want to kill me. You want my help."

"How can you help me?" she asked, and with two final steps she was standing right before him, one foot on his gun; the mouth of her gun snuggled against his stomach. "You can help me more than you already have, darlin'? I wish you'd tell me how."

Seth focused his eyes on her nose and parted his lips, darting his tongue out for a quick, nervous lick. "I know that I owe you big-time," he said in a rush. "I can help you get to Brazil. I'll drive you."

She turned her head to the side. *"How?"* she asked wispily. "How could I have trusted *you*? I don't trust anybody and I went and trusted a piece like you?"

It was hard to keep looking at her face, to not give it away: in his peripheral vision he saw the boy's mother making her stealthy way across the floor to the front door. The woman glided, hand outstretched for the knob. Her fingers touched the metal. Seth thought he could see the tendons and veins in her wrist jump as she started to twist it, but then Rae snorted and twisted her neck as if to relax a crick. "Stop right there, Sherry, or you'll have this man's murder on your conscience."

"Go! Run!" Seth shouted to the paused woman, and his eyes met Rae's and he didn't think he'd ever seen her so surprised. The corner of her mouth was hitched up as if to grin. "I'm not *all* shit," he told her.

1 : 1 0 a . m .

There must have been a dozen exits from the Sanctuary of Lady Rampart, but Welk seemed to be leading Joe to the least convenient of them. They had climbed two narrow flights of stairs, walked across a dripping wet fire escape attached to the rear exterior of the building, come back inside upon a crumbling brick vestibule whose floor was covered with a frayed green shag carpet, gone down a yellow hall of metal doors, and then a blank red hall, at the end of which Welk now shoved open a massive, buckled wood door marked with a glowing electric EXIT sign.

"Well this is what I kind of wanted you to see," Welk said matter-of-factly, stepping onto a balcony with Joe close behind him. He jerked his thumb away from him at waist level to indicate the view.

It was one of those sudden, disorienting moments. Joe felt

as though a landscape had descended from the sky and crashed down around him as he stood dumbly in place. He brushed past Welk, only faintly registering the touch of their forearms together, and went to the railing. "Oh, man," he said. "How's *this?*"

They were on the building's highest perch, up above all the adjacent rooftops, looking toward the Mississippi out over the Quarter. You could see brick courtyard walls speckled with broken shards of glass, dense little gardens, lazy swimmers in whitish blue swimming pools, alleyways spotlighted and dark, all of it from an angle that reminded Joe of being hunched over an old board game, deciding in which direction to move his piece. His eye fixed on a blazing courtyard where a lone cypress tree was strung with blue and purple lights that fluttered with the movement of the branches. In the top sliver of his vision he saw without actually focusing on them the still white beams bedecking ships docked on the banks of the river, and the electrified span of the bridge to Algiers. The sadness that had been flickering around the edges of his heart as he made his way through the building was now gone, replaced just like that with this mellow elation. He patted his thigh as if with a tambourine.

"You must come out here all the time," he said, leaning his head out as far as his neck would let it. A curly little warm breeze buttered the underside of his chin.

"Yeah, I do. I knew you'd like it."

"Who wouldn't?"

"Well, you'd be surprised."

Joe stepped back from the railing and bumped into the hard front of Welk, whose arm slithered around his neck with the elbow crook hitched just beneath Joe's chin. The big round muscles in the upper arm plumped up against the side of Joe's cheek and he sunk into a blissful reverie, romanticizing and burnishing their recent sex, which in fact had been kind of a contentious act alternating between Joe's laughter and Welk's grave raunchiness. Joe figured he had a lot to learn about the demeanor you put on when you were fucking.

Now Welk kissed him on the temple and loosened his grip, so his arm hung necklacy loose around Joe's neck. "You need to go home," he said, nibbling on Joe's T-shirt collar. "Little fish."

"Yeah." Joe sighed.

"The Jeep's out back."

"Cool. Okay."

Welk let go and walked over to the shadowy corner of the balcony. He twice kicked something metal, and suddenly, with a whoosh, a chain of ladder unrolled; within seconds, the bottom steps hit the ground with a muffled clang. Joe followed quickly and climbed easily down the four swaying rungs. The air became heavier and wetter during the descent, and by the time he jumped to the hard patio floor, he was sweating again; his T-shirt stuck to the small of his back.

"One night we need to sit out here and talk," Welk said, leaning his shins against a low wooden box the size of a coffin, in which a few stunted banana trees grew, their scorched leaves brushing the floor like monkey knuckles.

"Do you think we will?" Joe asked, mildly hopeful. "Like, are we going to ever see each other again?"

"Don't say that."

"You don't have to make me feel good. I mean, I feel good. You don't have to cover me with goo, though. I don't think it's like you're in love with me."

"No," Welk said nonchalantly, or fake-nonchalantly to piss Joe off, creaking open a metal door onto the thick of Burgundy St. and holding it open for him. "I'm not in love with you."

"Phew!" Joe staggered onto the sidewalk. This was another thing he needed to learn: questions you don't ask after you have sex; there were probably ten million of them.

Cars were crammed on both sides of the street, and up a block there was a clump of high-spirited chicks sporting around outside a bar. A dark green Jaguar cruised slowly past them, four precise notes of a Def Leppard song booming from its open windows: "Rock of ages . . ." Joe remembered the mysterious druidical figures from the MTV video, which they still showed every now and then for a laugh.

Welk made two halfhearted air guitar strums and pointed to the Jeep, just across the street. The passenger side was jammed against a street lamp, so Joe had to climb in on the driver's side. As he clambered across the poochy, slick red fabric, Welk pinched the back of his knee, and Joe looked over his shoulder, laughing with relief that it wasn't going to be a punitively serious kind of ride home.

After snapping open the plastic sheeting that covered the window openings, Welk settled in his seat. He held the steering wheel loosely, pumping the gas and rocking the Jeep back and forth until they had cleared the tight space. They putt-putted to the end of the block and turned a wide slow left on wide slow Esplanade, until they were underneath the tight canopies of thick-leaved tree limbs that spread over the street.

The Jeep stopped beneath a highway overpass for a red light. The signal shook frantically, as if at the end of a fishing line. In the diffuse beam of the Jeep's headlights, you could see the reds of people's eyes. They were sitting on the median grass beneath the highway, in abandoned cars, in shopping carts. Some of them smoked, some walked in circles, some sang. There was no route from the Quarter to the interstate that didn't take you through a blighted hellhole of abandoned people. Joe fixed his eye on the tan dog who scampered obliviously in and out of the headlight; he could have been a Country Day newbie's dog, trained to catch Frisbees. Sinking into his seat, Joe muttered, "Just go through the light, man. Downer."

Welk gave him a long appraising look, and then smiled and rushed the intersection, peeled tire rubber as he made a sharp right and spiraled them up the on-ramp. They rose up above the rooftops, the treetops, the post tops strung with electric wires, up into a sky of pit-stop, checked-flag fast-food banners and plump, delirious motel signs and, in the distance, the red-and-white security twinklers that outlined the derricks and catwalks and towers of old industrial complexes. Air gushed through the Jeep. Radios and thumping horns, the general rush of traffic, filled Joe's ears, and he wished that they could spiral up another on-ramp, and another, and another, until they were on the loudest, highest, fastest interstate, just thoughtlessly driving.

■

Halfway home, traffic slowed to pass the scene of an accident. Fierce white spotlights mounted on emergency vans bleached the skinny tree trunks on the far side of a ravine off to the right of the road. A truck had fallen headfirst into the gulley, and a tube of gray smoke rose from its cab. Facing the highway, on the near side of the ravine, was a second truck; its cab was on fire, its glass melting inward.

"My dad's dead," Joe said.

"I know," Welk said almost tonelessly. "Black Chris told me."

"He did?"

"He sort of took me off to the side, at the party."

"What did he say?"

"To treat you with respect, or whatever." Welk guffawed theatrically. "He's an all right guy. Sort of. But I had to kind of ask him what was his relation to you."

"My dad would *not* have wanted to know what I did tonight." He gave a small airy whistle and held his hand out in the air as if he expected to catch something. Overhead, jets approached, each with its distinct, massive wiggle, lowering its wheels for landing. Three of them in the sky, approaching at separate angles of descent, wings blinking and scarved with clouds.

"Well, probably most parents *don't* want to hear that shit— do they?"

"If I were, you know, a girl, I think my mom and I would talk about guys and stuff, but just the idea of like talking with her as *me* makes me want to puke. Like, if I were to tell her about the way it felt when you . . ."

"Well," Welk said, turning on Joe with a fat smile, "that's what I'm here for. Tell me how it felt."

"No, that's not the same. It's not, and you know it." As traffic picked up speed, he scooted down in his seat and settled in the orange night lull. Welk reached across and took his sweaty hand.

1:40 p.m.

Sherry had twice been mugged over lunch break as she made her way to the parking-garage ATM across the street from the hospital. Both assaults had taken less than a minute; their very briefness had frightened her most: the snarling face, the flash of gun in the sunlight, the shove, the pitiless threats— and then she was alone again, crying, her sleeve ripped, heel busted, her scared little voice repeating in her head, I could have been dead, I could have been dead.

Tonight was different. It was dragging on too long, and she felt in her heart a dull assurance that she'd prevail; she kept telling herself, I'm not going to die, I'm not going to die. She stood barefoot on top of a plain black $400 DKNY skirt she'd bought at Rubinstein Brothers on Canal Street over lunch one day this week. Her big toe was black from repeated stubbings and falls in her earlier fight with the woman who'd swarmed into her life out of nowhere, out of the fucking quiet night. Her arms and back ached from sitting at the kitchen, listening to the banshee lather at the mouth about her grand delusional "legacy" to New Orleans; she'd interrupted herself at a few dull spots to draw lewd but, Sherry wondered, possibly true innuendos about Joe, whom she claimed to have seen in a clutch at the NOAC with the man standing with them now in the lamplighted living room.

The three of them stood near the center of the room in a sort of triangle just to the side of the big, gauzily curtained bay window, through which you could see the black night just sitting there, patient. Babbling still, with private murmurs that Sherry didn't even try to hear, Rae Schipke held a gun in each hand, both pointed at Seth, as if she hadn't even enough contempt or fear of Sherry to draw a bead on her. The only mark on Schipke from their brawl around the house was the crusted-over little hole on the palm of her hand, the keychain nick the sight of which even now gave Sherry a little whiff of consolation.

Suddenly, as if she'd read her mind, Schipke turned on Sherry with a lunge and slipped one of the guns into Sherry's hand; Schipke placed her own hand on top of Sherry's then, and guided her finger to the trigger. She wheeled their joined gun hand upwards, aiming at Seth's face. The man kept blinking, trying not to flinch.

"Shoot him," Schipke said with just the subtlest little mean hint of frivolity in her voice.

Sherry began to open her hand, but Schipke squeezed it shut and jerked the gun an inch closer to Seth.

"I'm not going to shoot him," Sherry said. "You're not going to pull me into that." She didn't know if she had bundled up her passions and stuffed them deep in her bruised toes or *what*, but if this was pure terror, it was oddly sedating; if she closed her eyes, she was sure that she could fall asleep.

"Women are the ones," Schipke said, shrugging, bobbing their gun hand, "who won't curry favor with me. Women always give me the shits." She swung her second gun and shoved its mouth at Sherry's neck. "Now, Seth, tell this woman I'm serious."

"Rae," he said, squinting his eyes shut and flinching with every third or fourth word, "you're a fucking joke. You need to just walk out the door, get in your tired-ass minivan, and drive the hell off into the horizon."

"You don't add up to much," she whispered.

"I know," he said. "I don't mean much. What does that say about you, baby? That you dragged your business all the way over here to what—ambush me? Me?"

"Shut up."

"I'd almost be willing to die if I knew you'd shoot yourself, too. I'd have a hero's death if it meant you were erased."

"God *damn* you," Schipke said after a moment, and in the two seconds that it took her to pull the second gun away from Sherry's neck and thrust it back in Seth's face, Sherry made her move. She twisted the first gun from their shared grip, swung it up in a loose arc, and brought it down hard on the side of the woman's face. She pushed the round blowhole against the side of the woman's face and said with as much judo as she could muster the very words she remembered her first mugger saying to her. He'd been a young guy, barely a teenager, and he hadn't seemed scared at all.

"I'll do you," Sherry said, "I *will*, be*lieve* me I will." Then she looked up at Seth, who was smiling. "Go on," she said, "take the fucking gun out of her hand."

1 : 45 p . m .

It took just one sharp left off busy, flashy Old Metairie Road to enter into the deadly hush of Joe's neighborhood. A lot of times, upon coming home, Joe fought against the serenity by jumping around in his seat or fucking with the radio, but tonight, as the Jeep rounded the corner and glided down the slight hill toward his house, he looked around him with a forbearing smile and a shrug. "Park over here, skookieman," he said, pointing to the curb in front of Al Theim's house.

"Okay," Welk said, bringing the Jeep to a sputtering stop. "I like your house."

"Well this isn't my house." Then, automatically, he added: "A dick of a guy I used to like lives here."

"Should I kick his ass?"

"Al Theim? No, I mean Al Theim's whoever he is; I kind of in my mind turned him into a dick."

"Well, which house is yours?"

"Next door. The one that's all lighted up for a party; my mom is waiting up, I'm sure." He looked over at the house again, through a break in the shrubs along the perimeter of Al's lawn, and noticed the minivan parked beside Mom's car in the driveway. A little pinwheel of gladness began to spin inside his chest, and in a matter of seconds its good breeze had spread all throughout him. It was about time, he thought, that she had people over, even if only Chloris Devitt or Dave Sidey from the hospital for wine and pizza or whatever.

"So now we're here," Welk said.

"Looks like it."

"Hmmm." He put his fist against his chin to show Thinking, and Joe imitated the pose. They both gave a desultory chuckle and the moment dissolved away. "Well, Joe," Welk began, "I guess . . ."

"Oh, come on, don't say anything like a blessing or shit. No."

"Blessing? That's not what I wanted to—"

Joe interrupted again. "Thank you, man; I had a great night." He reached across the front seat to take hold of the hem of Welk's T-shirt, and with one fast, laughing lunge he peeled the fabric from Welk's torso and slipped his head beneath it, pressed his lips to the ridged, fuzzy warm belly and kissed its little button; he nudged his cheek against the skin for a moment longer as Welk patted his back and whispered sweet syllables, and then he pulled himself off the older boy's lap, unlatched the door, and stepped sideways onto the road, looking down at his Pumas.

■

Walking backwards across Al Theim's yard, each step sending the eggy smell of weed killer into the air, Joe watched the Jeep taillights dwindle, emberlike, and disappear. The street just lay there, all empty, but Joe had to admit, as cold of him as it may have been, that he didn't feel any kind of bereftness, no loneliness at all. As he came to a stop in the disputed territory between the Theim lawn and his own—a weedy strip that neither family cared to mow—he began to cry a few elated tears and hiccup a sob. He turned on his heel and looked at his house and wiped the burning liquid slivers from his lower lids. This is our house, he said, with a little corny surprise, to himself and to the little part of his mother that he carried inside him. Its exterior was white brick and pinkish white aluminum siding that was fake-mottled to resemble stucco, and if snobby people had it in their icy asshole hearts to call it tacky then Joe guessed they'd just go ahead and do it. It was still the house that his mom and dad had always promised him when they sat down to dinner or breakfast or plopped in front of the TV at one of the many, dozens, trillions of apartments in which they'd lived in Florida, Alabama, Pennsylvania, New Mexico. The House We'll Have had taken on its own mythology: it would have elevators and fountains, an aviary, a gym, a home theater, a sewing room, a fire pole, and Mom and Daddy would actually be there, be home; their jobs and the family bills wouldn't demand such frantic attention. Funny, Joe thought, sniffling and wiping the back of his hand across his cheek, they didn't want him to grow up in an apartment. *Why?* Each one in which they'd lived had been fine with him; more than fine, even: regular, comfortable, smelling like home, with enough bedrooms and a kitchen and a bathroom or two. What about the one in a tower near the beach, the one with the saltwater swimming pool and an ice-cream shop in the lobby? That place had been swankier than a sixed-out Miami Beach hotel. It did tear him the fuck up when he let himself remember that his parents had been way down hard on themselves for living where they lived. Leave that alone, he thought to himself; they should just leave that alone; they shouldn't waste their time on *that.* The world was this sickening, amazing, rapid-fire place where you had to kind of dig your heels into the ground and just say, What the fuck, it's too late, and not dwell on the shit you couldn't fix up.

Despite the pinkish orange clouds at the fringes of the sky down near the vanishing line, giving a warm illusion to the way the night looked, it was actually getting stupid cold out; it hadn't been this chilly since one or two April deviations. Joe rubbed his palms down his thighs as if to smooth away the goose bumps and then, as he began to lower his butt to the grass for a sit, for a little bit longer of solitude before he faced his mom, he heard soft footsteps coming toward him. He looked into the dark hollow between the houses and saw first a white tank top, then bright green Filas, and then the rest of Al Theim, strutting even-shouldered toward him, head thrown back and smiling.

"Joe," Al whisper-called. "Little Joe Keith, where's your dang sheep? Let me take a peep. Cheep cheep cheep."

"Al," Joe whispered back happily, "what's your stupid ass sayin'?"

"Hey."

"Hey."

Al broke into a crouching run, one bouncy strong stride after the next, and pitched himself into the grass beside Joe; as he fell, elbows first, he made a little private stupid face that Joe had always thought was one of the ten coolest things in New Orleans, all tonguey and curly eyed, shy. The usual Al Theim soapy smell wafted electrically across the space between them, and Joe tried to discreetly sniff in a liter. "What're you doing?" Al asked. "Where've you been?" He inched closer, digging his elbows into the grass, until he was right there, almost touching. "You don't even want to know how bored I was."

"I kind of can guess."

"Yeah, I saw you out my window and I had to come down. You know?"

"Well, who wouldn't? *Jok*ing."

"So what'd you do?"

Joe nudged his shoulder—imperceptibly, he hoped—against Al's elbow and looked down the length of his nose at the guy's tight shoulder, on which a new little hump of muscle bulged. "I don't know what I did."

"Come *on*, give me like one little thrill."

"Man, I've had a long night," he said in a voice he knew was implausibly grown-up. He chuckled two short syllables in compensation. "It's cool to just hang here with someone normal."

"Dude," Al said somberly, "*what?*"

"Oh, damn, I don't know."

"What? What?!" He flopped his hand down on the part of Joe's arm where the biceps should have been and squeezed. "Tell me! Dude, you're skinny! What?"

"Shhh. I don't want my mom to hear me." He tried to bat Al's hand away. "I'm so late. I was down in the Quarter." He flopped back onto the wet grass, which immediately began to soak through his T-shirt.

Another tight squeeze, and Al whispered, "This late?"

"Yeah."

"Who with? Wyatt K.? Who?"

Joe squeezed his eyes shut and sucked his lips inside his mouth before blurting, "Can I tell you the truth without freaking you?"

"Am I gonna be grossed out? Don't say anything gooey or shit, okay?"

" 'Kay."

"Well am I gonna be grossed out?"

"You might." Joe laughed.

"Really!"

"Shhh."

"Okay."

"I met this cool dude who's from that orphanage trial on TV or whatever."

Al dropped his face into the grass, moaning theatrically, and then flipped onto his back without seeming to use his arms. Finally, after Al's silence lingered uncomfortably on and on, Joe whispered, "Hey, Al?"

"Did you, like, *fuck?*"

"Um, yeah?"

"Really." Al rolled onto his stomach and then his back again, so that there were now two spaces between him and Joe. "So that's the way it really is, huh. Like that?" His voice trailed off shyly on the last word.

"It really is."

"Wow."

"I guess."

With a sudden burst of energy, he elbow-crawled his way back, setting his face right beside Joe's. "You know I'm not that way," he whispered, "or not officially, anyway."

"Well I didn't sign a contract, dude."

Without even smiling, Al said, "Whoa," and hitched his chin on Joe's shoulder. "So if I'm lonely or whatever then maybe we can sort of unofficially do whatever."

Joe looked up at the sky for a second, but the stars made him dizzy. "No sir."

"I saw the way you looked at—"

"You need to get yourself in circulation. I know some cool

girls. I can actually guarantee you that some girls I know would be totally into some buff nice guy like you."

"Who?" Al asked, his lips now brushing the side of Joe's cheek and the top of his chest holding Joe's shoulder to the grass. "What girls? You would introduce me?"

"I totally would."

"Tell me about them," Al's dreamy soft voice murmured right beside Joe's ear.

■

Sirens whistled in the distance, but the night was untroubled. Al Theim's head and shoulders rested comfortably heavy across Joe's belly, and Al's mouth blew raspy little snores. Joe himself was loose-faced, just barely awake. He was in a sort of warm, buzzy, worn-out, complacent temper. Actually, he wasn't even himself. There was an empty space where his insides had been—room for anyone, anything, to come fill him up. For minutes at a time he'd become the grass beneath his head, or the trees wiggling against the sky, or a car passing so slowly that its tires crackled for an eternity on the gravel. For a while he was even Al Theim, and sort of enjoyed the experience of resting his head on top of Joe Keith.

As the sirens grew closer, louder, he slowly opened his eyes and let his gaze rest on the front window of his house. He blinked deliberately, and thought he could see his mother through the front window. When he closed his eyes, he smiled.

He could see her. She was young, bony, a bit stooped over when she walked. She had wide plump lips the color of nipples, and pale green eyes. Her eyebrows were blunt little dashlike things, bleached and then penciled dark, and her long, perfectly straight hair was the color of cocoa powder, fresh from the tin. How old was she? She was twenty-eight, or thirty, or whatever, that age, and Joe wasn't even born. She hadn't even thought of him yet.

Lights flashed across the front of the house in a whorl of shadowy white and blue, and Joe brought himself swiftly and forcibly awake. He sat up, dumping Al onto the grass.

"What?" Al asked feebly. "*What?*"

Joe didn't answer. He tried to look past the reeling bursts of white siren light that were reflected in the windows and making movies on the aluminum siding. When he saw his mother kind of staggering down the sidewalk toward the driveway, he got a gallop in his heart and rose to his feet. He watched a cop put his arm around Mom's shoulders, and there were other cops in the driveway and going into the house and talking into their hand-helds. It looked like three dozen cops with flashes of light swirling across their backs. Four dozen. But that was too many, Joe knew. He was in a state of unclearness, and didn't trust his own eyes. He stood on weak legs in the grass. "Mom!" he called, watching her talk to first one cop and then the next. "Mom!" His voice was swallowed up in the sirens.

Why don't you look over here, Mom?

Why don't you come to me?

Why don't you hold me just one more time before you let me go?

About the Author

Ben Neihart grew up in Florida and Lancaster, Pennsylvania. He got his M.A. from Johns Hopkins University in 1994, and was also educated at George Washington and the University of Southern Mississippi. His stories have appeared in *The New Yorker.* This is his first novel. He lives in Baltimore.